THE GARDEN MAZE

ISAAC ANDERSON

NORLAND PRESS

THE DUKE OF PURG

The puppet smiled on the striped stage. Bright red circles stood on its cheeks and its jingling hat lopped on its head in a lazy point. It shook a stick in its hand. The other puppet never saw him coming.

"Punch! Punch!"

Children pointed. Cheered. Some tried to warn the other puppet even as they laughed. "He's there, THERE!"

The oblivious, fat puppet cocked his head and asked in a nasalized breath, "Nehhh?"

Punch thumped his paper skull, knocking his hat into the giggling children below.

A Knight and his Squire watched all this from afar. The man stood tall and rail-thin, dressed in polished leather and wool dyed to green. The boy wore simple garments, gray and girded with a wide belt. His face was thin and freckled beneath his nest of dark hair.

"And how culture rots," the Knight said, twitching his mustache and turning to view the wide field with its bright, billowing tents. People of all sorts milled about, some to view an act or feat, and others eager to spend whatever coin they'd mined from their neighbor's pockets.

The Century Fair was certainly a sight.

Folk had come from every corner of Norland to see it. To see if the stories their grandfathers had spoken were true. To gaze in wonder at the towers built in a day and the multitude of flags raised to such heights that they roared like an ocean over their heads.

There were folk from the Timber Drop Mountains and the Desert of Rot. He saw the hulking boar-beasts and the goblins who rode them. He heard the bellows of the war-men as they called their challenges and struck deathblows in the painted arenas as crowds cheered their favorites.

For five hundred years, the Century Fair blossomed here among the ruins of Purg, Norland's first kingdom.

The Knight turned back to the children as they roared with glee. Punch had turned the other puppet's shirt overhead, revealing dotted undershorts.

At his side, his Squire spoke. "Couldn't we... get a little closer," he said. "The Viscount said we had the evening to ourselves, after all."

"And such a gift one should not waste on puppets," the Knight said.

He turned again to scan the crowd. He looked for nobles, merchants, anyone who might want an audience with the Viscount—currently drinking himself into oblivion with his "friends" inside a thrumming red tent, center of the field.

A tug at his sleeve.

"Sir," the Squire said.

"Hush now, I'm working."

"Yes, but—"

"Do you enjoy living in service to the Viscount? If we're clever, we can get out from under the bumbling oaf. Find a real pennant to fly."

The Squire pulled again at his arm, "But Sir…"

"What, blast it?"

The Knight spun, following the Squire's gaze to see the purple, blanched face of the Viscount. The over-flowing man stumbled for them over the turf like a turkey dipped in pudding.

"Sir Knight!" The Viscount cried. He gurgled a conspiratorial laugh and took the Knight's shoulder, whispering into his beard in a bounding, drunken voice. "How would you like to make us a bit of money, eh?"

The Knight unwound the man from his person. In all their travels over the past few months, the Viscount showed interest in only two things: wine and coin. And preferably mixed.

"Money, my lord?" the Knight said.

"Yes, yes." The Viscount ran his arm over his mouth, dragging his lip. "I said that, didn't I? Oh, you really should try this ale under the—"

The Viscount blinked and laughed in a blasting shout. "Is that Punch? Oh, I love Punch!"

The Viscount led them toward a dark tent set aside from the festivities, nearer to the towering ruins of Purg. Their master gurgled a laugh and said, "My name opens doors, yes? This shall impress you, sir Knight."

The man stumbled. Only the Knight's steady hand kept the fat fool from burying his face in the sod. He felt heat boil up within him. He'd been nothing more than a babysitter for months. Were not for the oath he had made to this lout's father…

He breathed. "I am constantly impressed, my lord."

The tent loomed before them like a mouth. Its ropes and ties had been dipped in the darkest of paint. Its canvas held tight on its poles and gave it a crown of horns. The thing looked like a shadow risen from hell.

"I met one of the man's wards today," the Viscount said, oblivious to the Knight's hand at his arm. "He's not one to accept an audience lightly, you know. But when I challenged the poor fool," he barked a laugh, "like a hook in the mouth of a fish!"

The Knight smiled, and a short man ducked from the tent to wave them in.

"You have a talent for this, my lord," the Knight said. "Making friends."

"Careful now," the Viscount said, shrugging away. "You've such a grip!"

"My apologies." the Knight turned an eye to his Squire and tipped his head toward their bumbling master.

The boy slipped closer to the man, hand near the skinning knife hidden in his belt. It was a strategy they'd perfected, should the worst rear its head.

A short man stopped them at the shadowed entrance. His block of a brow jutted far over his eyes and his hairy arms came from his sides, palms open. "Your weapons, my masters," he said. "The Duke allows no sword but his own, beyond."

The Knight slipped his sword from his belt and helped the Viscount with his own. The Squire's hidden knife remained at his side.

The short man took the blades in his arms like a load of kindling, and led them forth.

"Fear not the cobra," he said. "She shall let you pass."

And as they ducked—indeed—the Knight spied the diamond-patterned skin of a wide serpent overhead. It circled the whole of the tent like a living curtain and moved as a sleeper rolls in bed. He could not say where the creature's head lived above. It was dim in the Duke's tent, despite the lanterns strewn about.

The place smelled of mint.

Rugs and pelts covered the floor, and velvet curtains formed a little enclave, sealing the space beyond their view. A table with silver plates and candles and another holding nothing but a stone basin of brackish water were the room's only decoration. A man stood between them.

The Duke of Purg had piercing eyes and a wide smile. He flashed gapped teeth in a grin.

"The Viscount of Velay!" he said and crossed the myriad of rugs and skins to greet them. "So pleased to meet you. It sorely pained me to hear of your father's death."

"Don't be. He was rich!" The Viscount pulled a smile of his own, but it looked frogish. "In all our wide travels, I have not seen an equal to your festivities, good lord." The Viscount overstepped the shaggy pelt of a boar and checked his boot against the tent pole. The Squire hurried to steady him, but the drunk man hardly noticed, keeping his arm outstretched to the Duke, but the smiling man kept his hands folded behind his back.

"I've heard tale you have a champion to fetch the Prize from the Maze of Purg?" the Duke said.

"That I do, my lord." The Viscount wobbled back and clapped the Knight's arm. "This man! This. Man. May I announce, The Last Knight of Norland. He served my father these ten years and in all that time we've not feared enemy nor peril." The Viscount took a breath. "This is the man for your maze!"

The Duke of Purg turned his smile to the Knight. Studied him up and down. "You speak true?" he asked the Viscount. "This man is of those mighty men?"

The Viscount wobbled. "Of course! I know he's a bit of an old goat, but this goat can still kick and bite as well as any other!"

The Duke's smile never left his face, but it did change. Now, it stretched thin over his teeth as he regarded the Knight.

"Do you know of our honored tradition, sir knight? Of the Maze? It is not a story many know. The common folk come for the Century Fair—an old tradition, but there is an older one which forms its root."

He crossed the rugs and waved to his ornate curtains and their swirling maze of stitching. "The Ancients of Purg were a proud people. A great people. The first of Norland as the story goes, but they fell long ago. Disappeared. Without them, time and war and change made ruins of their cities and wonders—everything reduced to rubble—save for the Garden Maze."

The Knight nodded. "I know of the tale. Every hundred years, the Maze of Purg opens."

"No!" the Duke said. "The maze is always open, but should you enter you'd find yourself ejected far before the end. Indeed, the challenge then is to find your way deeper. This is impossible. The Maze rejects all and keeps its treasure for itself. But tomorrow," his eyes flashed, "the Maze shall Open to the worthy."

He stretched his arms wide and the coils of the cobra stretched and folded. From the darkness above the Viscount, the Knight spied a pair of sharp, golden eyes.

"Tomorrow, Purg awakens. Only then is the way made to the prize hidden in its heart. Only then can the wisest brave its depths. Are you such a man, sir knight?"

The Knight frowned, beard scrunching into his mouth. In his vision's edge, he spied again the glassy eyes of the cobra moving above them.

"I served under Kragmael of the Hundred Hands," he said. "I marched upon the Cliffs of Night in the Siege Year. I destroyed the Giants of Timberdrop and struck down Widow-Wyrms as they feasted upon corpses in the Desert of Rot."

A wink of fangs above, then a snap like the wringing of a cloth. The Knight flashed his hand and seized the hooded serpent, shutting fast its jaw. It mewled—a quiet sound—as all about its length it squirmed and shook the tent.

A twist of his gloved hand and a crackling like so many twigs stilled the serpent forevermore.

The Knight raised a wiry brow. "I fear not your maze."

The Duke smiled all the wider.

In their own modest tent (set up directly behind the Viscount's brightly colored monstrosity), the Knight flashed his blade over the pitted stone in his hand. The smell of the crackling sparks was enough to make him sneeze but he tweaked his nose, snuffling it away. He ran the edge of his knife again over the stone.

At the tent's flap, his Squire poked his wiry head through. "Master!" he cried. "There is a man here who would speak to you!"

The Knight looked down his angled nose at the boy. "What sort of man?"

"Old, sir. Very much so. Older than even you."

The Knight bristled but held his tongue. He waved for the tent flap. "Bring him in, then."

The man who ducked into their little tent stood scarcely taller than the boy who led him. His face was a guide of wrinkles and his nose pugged beneath hooded, silvery eyes.

"My dear good knight, can you see me?" the man asked.

The Knight said, "I do."

From beneath his robes, the old man revealed a book bound from leather and bark. The sharp smell of ink and the husky aroma of dried pine filled the tent.

"I spent my days as a young man chasing after the legends of Purg," he said, pressing the book into the Squire's arms. His sightless eyes found the Knight. It was like beholding a creature from the eternal deep.

"Here are the secrets of that ancient tongue. They shall guide you and protect you from the traps within the Maze as you quest for the center."

The Knight knelt to better see the man. His blind face fluttered, searching in vain for the Knight's eyes. The old man's mouth dipped open, never closing. "You are a knight?" he asked, emotion coloring his voice. "A Knight of Norland?"

"I served beneath Kragmael during the Year of Siege," the Knight said.

The old man drew a breath and dropped to his knees. "My liege," he said. "I would ask a blessing of you."

But the Knight shook his head. "The only blessing I can give is my continued breath upon this earth. For each I draw, I live for the sake of Norland."

These words had waited, ready on his lips, even as the old man entered. Everywhere the Knight had traveled, he'd meet men such as these: scared and broken from war, desperate for one last glimmer of what the world had been before it had turned to dust before their eyes.

The words served their effect (as they always did), calming the old face and bringing tears to wobble in his sightless eyes. "Please, accept my gift," he said and patted the bound book in the Squire's arms. "May it make your way all the lighter as you travail the Maze, noble Knight."

Then he tottered out and away, leaving them in the dark of the tent.

"Master," the Squire asked, heaving the ancient book, "How shall I pack this? It is heavier than it should be, by right."

The Knight waved his arm. "We will not take it," he said. "The old man was a relic of war. Mad, most like. He's never set a toe in that maze. You heard what the Duke told us: it hasn't truly opened in a hundred years. Anything you'd find in that book would be ravings. To study them would be to risk madness yourself."

The Squire left the weathered tome on the grassy floor of the tent. But as the Knight took his leave to find food and drink, the boy tucked the book away, wrapping it in a saddle blanket.

THE WAGER

The Garden Maze shadowed the edge of the ruins of Purg, forming an impassable border between the Century Fair and the dark, basalt coasts of the Grey Sea. Its leafy walls rose twenty feet high and as the Knight and Squire looked on it with gaped mouths, they could hear the harsh buzz of ocean air cutting over its heights.

The Duke walked at their side. "A sight, yes?"

The Knight could only agree. Its leaves lay perfect and flat, creating a wall as fine as marble. Living marble, at that. "Do none see to this?" The Knight asked, waving a gloved hand to the towering hedge. "Surely there is a *gardener* who tends this!"

The Duke shook his head. "The ancients of Purg were wise in many things, the Maze above all. No man maintains this place."

The Viscount ambled behind, head in his hands and grumbling. He looked to have spent the night in a pan of ale. "How long will it take to run this maze of yours?" the drooping man asked. "An hour? A day?"

The Duke shrugged and smiled back at the man. "It has been a hundred years. I know not much for certain, except the Maze of Purg will not part from its riches easily."

"Have any succeeded?" the Squire asked.

"Of course!" The Duke said, turning his smile to the boy. "Every Century, victors emerge from the Maze, each with a treasure from Purg's ancient riches. If you prevail whatever awaits, you shall never want for comfort again."

The Viscount squinted his reddened face at the smiling duke. He scratched at his chin. "And what do *you* get from this?"

The Duke said, "All I ask is for you to bring not only one prize but *two*. Should you prevail, I shall give you the pick of them, but one shall belong to me."

The Viscount frowned. Bit his lip. "What if we strike a bargain? A wager?"

"What have you to bargain with?"

"My noble Knight of Norland!" the Viscount cried. "If he can return before the moon grows full—three days—I get both treasures."

"And if he should tarry, I will receive this man into my service and my allotted tribute?" The Duke's smile shrank to its thinnest. The man brought together his fingertips and mulled as they walked.

It was all the Knight could do to keep his laughter within his heart. If this bargain came to pass, he knew which way he should wager.

Oh, to at last be free of that drunken oaf! To no longer swat pickpockets away from the man's coat or listen to another night of drunken conspiracy. He could at last hold his head high and in honor, pledging his service to one worthy of the last Knight of Norland.

The Duke of Purg said, "I need a new protector. The Cobra was exotic, yes, but it's only right that her vanquisher should take her place." His smile returned all the brighter. "I accept this."

The Duke halted before a stone jutting from the perfect flat of the hedge wall, the only sign of disorder for leagues. It rose high over their heads and as the Duke reached out a hand to touch its smooth face; the Knight saw in its shadow a dark cut into the garden beyond.

"This is the only way in," the Duke said to the Viscount. "I must warn you, it can often take many days to travail the maze. The odds rest with me."

The Viscount smiled his frogish smile. "You underestimate the Knight of Norland, good sir. Both prizes shall be mine."

The Knight said nothing, smoothing his face to absolute calm as he and the boy stepped beyond the stone and into the Garden Maze.

Take a moment and consider the ancient kingdom of Purg.

Perhaps you've visited it in your travels and seen the aged spires and rocky coast. Perhaps you've climbed the rubble of its walls and felt the springy moss growing here and there. Many have looked out over the rumbling break of the waves and into the grey sea beyond.

Purg had been a nation both wise and foolish. They built tall and wide, covering the plains, touching the coastline with cities joined by stone roads and clapping flags. To look at them was to behold a shining gem, as the histories might say.

And surely, this must be true. Even their ruins held beauty.

And there was the *Garden Maze* itself. Such a deceptive thing to call it. True, it was a garden, but not one you'd want to visit. Black thorns grew in the hedges unseen beneath the wide, waxy leaves. Flowers of all sorts had once beautified the maze, but a black, drooping flower had taken the hedge over in years past and choked out all others.

The curious smell of soil after a rain smothered the air and coated the Knight's throat as they walked, sun shining brightly overhead. They stopped at a crossway and the Knight peered at his bracer. He'd marked every turn upon it with chalk.

Four hours they'd been walking, and not a single dead end. He felt he would have surely happened upon several before the sun reached its peak. Yet here they were, dabbing their eyes and pulling careful sips at their canteens. The perfume of those bloody flowers made his head buzz.

"Master," the Squire said, rubbing his eyes. "We've gone left the past three turns. Shouldn't have we... I don't know how to say..."

"Run into our previous path?"

"Yes, that's what I mean. I've been counting my steps, and I'm sure we should have hit a wall in the hedge."

The boy turned a circle. "Or perhaps we are on one of our previous paths?" he said.

"Impossible." The Knight glanced again at the chalk marks on his bracer. "I've noted every turn. And look," He waved an arm at the ground behind them.

"We've been leaving more sign than a bloodied ox. If we'd happened upon our trail we'd have surely noticed so".

The Squire wet his lips and gazed up at the high wall of the hedges surrounding them. "I wish we had a way around those horrid thorns. I'd climb up and know for sure where we've been."

"I don't care about that," the Knight said. "All I want is to find a bloody *dead end*. I'm tempted to trace our steps back, if only to find one!"

The Squire nodded toward the turn. "Perhaps another left will do it. Surely it must be a dead end. You can't turn left four times in a row and not hit a wall."

So they turned left, but there was no wall to be found.

What they came across was an ivy-covered stone.

The Knight halted. The river-rock gravel under his boots squeaked as he knelt to push aside the ivy. Beneath it, a polished stone pushed out like a milk-white face. On it, the most curious of writings danced beneath the Knight's eyes.

"Can you read it?" the Squire asked.

The Knight scrunched his face. "I spent three years serving under the Head Counter of Oss when I was a lad no older than yourself. I learned a great deal of language."

He tried to trace the swirl of the letters with a finger, but the words carved on the stone seemed to wriggle, fighting at any attempt to be understood. He brought a knuckle to his lip and scowled.

"We go right," he said, pointing the way. "For if we turn *left*, a mass of living, writhing hair shall set upon us!"

The Squire jumped. "Heaven preserve us!"

"Indeed. Step to, boy. And keep your blade at the ready. There might not be a mass of tangles waiting to drown us ahead, but we should be ready for anything."

The Knight drew his sword and the Squire his skinning knife. They paused at the turn, knuckles turning white, then rounded the corner.

The Knight and Squire stumbled into a colonnade of modern art.

THE GALLERY OF PURG

The gravel gave way to cut marble, and the garden opened up before them in a wide oval. Ancient, grooved pillars rose above the towering walls of the maze and in the center sat an ivied pavilion with open sides. All around, hanging from the hedge maze walls in pedantic lines, were paintings of all sorts.

Could this be it? The Maze's center, so soon?

The Knight took a slow step, his boot clicking on the marble. He could hear the bubbling of a fountain somewhere deeper in the maze, and as he peered about, he saw more paths than ever leading out into the maze. He let his sword drift down from his shoulder till the tip kissed the marble with a musical tink.

"Those horrible flowers are gone," the Squire said. The boy paced toward the ivy-dressed pavilion, his skinning knife lulling harmlessly at his side. "And look," he pulled a deep breath through his mouth, relished it. "It's like my head's clear and I can reason again!"

The Knight wet his lips, turning around. "Yes, I feel the same. Strange. I didn't feel confused before, but now I'm clear as a bell."

A voice rose to meet them. "Welcome, good sirs, to the Gallery of Purg," it said in a slow drone.

Knight and Squire turned to see a small figure standing before one of the twisting marble paths leading out from the colonnade.

He wore a dark suit with tails trailing behind him and a navy vest with buttons the same color as the polished marble surrounding them. The single most extraordinary thing about him was his tall, brown ears and white, hanging teeth.

The Rabbit looked them over with half-lidded eyes and a sniff, scanning their muddied shoes and sweat-stained shirts. He moved his lips, falling somewhere between a smile and a sneer. "Enjoying the maze, are we?"

The Knight had never come across a talking rabbit in his journeys. Ravens, yes, and once a dolphin, but never a crea-ture of fur and tail. He steadied himself where he stood and nodded down to the creature.

"What is this place?" he said. "Are you friend or foe?"

The rabbit lifted one eyebrow. "As I've already stated, good knight, this is the Gallery of Purg. An exposition displaying the many wondrous works of those ancient and most wise folk." He tipped a little bow, dragging the tails of his suit. "I'm no foe of yours, sir. And—I must say—you are a cut above the usual raffle I entertain. The last tour I gave, why, they hardly showed any appreciation for our collection. Lower breeding, I'm afraid to say."

The rabbit pandered toward one painting. "Take this piece," he said. "I fear only those with some form of higher learning can truly grasp its beauty."

The Knight beheld it.

A single blue dot rested on the naked canvas. Beneath it, written in a small and tidy hand, hung one word.

Hollow

The rabbit rolled an eye toward the Knight. "How does this piece affect you?"

The Knight pulled at his mustache. Turned his head. "This is a work based upon the human experience."

"Well, of course it is," the rabbit said, flicking a bit of dust from his navy vest. "Nearly everything is a human experience. Tell me what you feel when you look at it."

The Squire ventured a guess. "I feel lonely," he said.

The rabbit shrugged his shoulders. "At face value, yes, I can see how you might feel so. I was hoping for something a bit more perspicacious."

The Knight jut his chin and lifted a finger. "This was painted by a man very young, while feigning the wisdom of one very old."

The rabbit's ears twitched, and his brows met high on his forehead. He nodded slow.

"Very interesting," he said. "This was painted by a young man, a prince of Purg once-upon-a-time." He squinted an eye at the Knight. "You possess insight, sir."

The Knight simply moved his gaze to the next painting on display in the colonnade, this one of a single hand floating in space above a basin of water sparkling with hidden silver.

"But this one speaks to me more, I think," the Knight said. "We spend our lives searching for things. Things we lose or things that are lost of us. Here, even the hand that seeks loses itself in the searching."

The rabbit scuttled to the Knight's side. "My, my," he said, a genuine smile touching his face. "You have some culture indeed."

The Squire looked on as the Knight and rabbit moved further and further into the gallery, each sly in their conversation and muted in their praise of whatever work of art they stood before. The Squire dared to tug at his master's sleeve.

"We have stayed here long," he said, wearily eying the rabbit as he strolled deeper into the marbled maze, brushing aside the greying leaves of the maze with the tails of his suit.

"It is a strange thing, this rabbit," he said. "Perhaps he means to lead us about this gallery till the death of all things? Could this be the trap the old soldier warned of?"

But the Knight brushed him away. "We've spent many long months addling our minds with that sop of a Viscount. What with those horrid Punch puppets and his drunken masquerades. I haven't fed the old grey-cells in so long, I feared them wasted away to butter. But this," he roved his arm to the collected works, looming over them like a colorful jury, "It wasn't the flowers, my boy, that had us muddled. We've been muddled for ages! This house of culture is better than the sweetest of fresh air to the mind."

"Precisely," the rabbit spoke, rounding back to meet them. "There is no finer wine of knowledge than the Gallery of Purg." He lifted a paw toward a new path in the maze and ushered them forth.

"You are a true aesthete, good Knight, and I do not show this particular piece to just anyone."

He huddled closer, and the Knight knelt to study the rabbit's face eye-to-eye. The creature held up his paws before him as if to describe the form of a forgotten treasure.

"What lays just beyond this hedge is the jeweling achievement of the Lost People of Purg. A triumph. All other works are spittle set next to this true masterpiece."

The Knight drank the rabbit's words, his eyes growing brighter and brighter. A masterpiece beyond any created before it! The Knight rose to follow the rabbit as he bounded in, but the Squire tugged again at his sleeve.

"Master," he begged. "This creature has watched us all along, wetting his lips like we were pigs on a spit! Please, the day is gone and we've been led through the maze with no thought of finding our way out again. Let us leave this place!"

But the Knight pulled his sleeve from his Squire's grasp. "You sound like a fretful maid," he said. "There is nothing to fear in this place. I know danger, boy. And what have we to fear of a rabbit? Besides, this could be the prize we seek!"

With that, the Knight rounded the corner, his boots clicking upon the marble.

Bodies crowded the viewing room. Men and Women of all sorts stood shoulder to shoulder. At first, the Knight could not catch sight of what held them entranced.

"Follow me," the rabbit said. "There is some space just ahead."

The Knight pushed his way through the crowd, muttering apologies as he did. They paid him no notice.

"I am a bird beholding a mountain," muttered one man.

"It's as if I am a seed in the endless blue of the sky," said another.

An old woman dressed in a sleeping gown said, "It makes me feel as if I am a little girl again, roaming father's apple orchard."

Each voice sounded heavy, some croaked as they spoke, but everyone carried quivering awe in their words. The Knight doubled his effort to push ahead.

"It's just here," the rabbit said from underfoot. "A few steps more."

Another tug at his sleeve, but the Knight ignored it. His Squire could fret on his own. The Knight wanted to see, needed to see. He pressed past a woman in dark silks and jewels, and a man as round as a beetle dabbing his eyes with a red cloth. "I've never.... I've never seen," the man kept repeating.

Then the Knight froze.

Shuddered.

He lost his feet from beneath him and dropped to his knees as he gazed at the painting.

The rabbit's voice came close by his ear. His breath was warm. "Behold it, good Knight. Look upon perfection."

"Yes," the Knight said, mouth agape. "A masterpiece."

The rabbit whispered closer, cupping the Knight's ear with a paw. "What do you see? Have you words for it? Few ever do."

The Knight tried, but it was like grasping for colors you've never seen or music you've never heard. He couldn't speak, only gape like a fish beholding the sun.

The Squire had frozen in his steps long before the Knight dissolved into the crowd of onlookers. He could see nothing beyond. Every hair on his neck shivered and stood on end.

He felt as if worms coiled within his stomach.

"Oh, we should have turned left!" he said, pulling at his cap. "A mass of writhing hair would surely be better than this!" Hair you could at least cut—the Squire reasoned—and short of burying his skinning knife into the rabbit's chest, he didn't know what was to be done. One thing above all stood out to him: he mustn't look upon the painting. Whatever it was, it would swallow him as a maelstrom swallows a listing ship.

But he could not leave his master.

The Squire hurried to the crowd, arm thrown over his face. He ran into their legs, knocking some of them over into sprawling piles. One man, dressed up in long robes with bands around his thin wrists, reached for the Squire's collar.

"Have you no respect for this place?" the man hissed.

The Squire risked a look at the man as he tore away. His face was gaunt, withered to bone and skin. He shot out a skeletal hand.

"Have you no respect?"

The Squire swallowed a scream and dove deeper into the writhe of the crowd, again pressing his arm to his eyes. Voices rose in alarm all around him. Hands tried to seize him, tearing at his hair and scratching at his neck, but their grips were weak from years wasting away in the Rabbit's gallery.

But then claws dug into the Squire's chest and the hissing voice of their guide spat in his face.

"I can cast you to the Roses," he said, renewing his grip. "Have you come across them yet? They'll make you beg for your death, lad. Beg for it."

Then the rabbit's voice smoothed, but the claws in the Squire's skin dug all the deeper. "Wouldn't you rather look upon perfection? Isn't that better?"

The rabbit's claws found the Squire's arm now, scratching burning lines from elbow to wrist. Biting. Trying anything to bring his eyes to see the painting.

The Squire lashed out with his skinning knife and the rabbit was gone like he'd never been. He could hear the shrieking rage of their guide, cursing, spitting, and howling a throat-ripping scream into the sky.

The Squire ran, holding out his free arm to feel his way. He bumped into the Knight. The man ignored him, only puttering under his breath as he gazed up at the rabbit's trap.

The Squire's fist touched rough canvas. The dried, looping oils crunched under his fingers like autumn leaves.

The rabbit screeched as the Squire brought his knife across the painting. Again and again and again.

Then, like someone snapping their finger in the air, The Knight blinked. He ran his sleeve over his face and found his eyes burned and watering.

"I... I saw Kragmael," he sputtered and was surprised to find he was weeping great, pulling sobs. "Kragmael... I left him there. Just left him there..."

The Squire took hold of his collar. "Master, please wake up! We must leave this place!"

The Knight pushed him away and rose on shaking legs. "Of course we have to get out of here!" he roared and took in the viewing room, seeing it for what it was at last.

Emaciated men and fading women cowed around them, gazing listlessly, confused and grumpy like sleepers.

A frail woman dressed in rose-colored and dusty finery said in a shaking voice, "But... it was so beautiful. Perhaps we can stitch it back together?"

The bone-thin mob rushed for the remains of the painting, taking up the tattered pieces and pressing them back to the frame. The Knight and Squire jumped to get out of the way. One of the weakened souls, the same who had grappled with the Squire, set his deep-set eyes against them.

"No respect," he growled through his fading teeth.

The Knight and Squire watched as they scrambled to fix the painting. Neither had ever seen such a sight. It brought a nauseating itch to the back of the Knight's throat.

He pressed a hand to the boy's back. "Run. Don't look back."

"But where? We are lost! The rabbit led us—"

"Anywhere is better than here!"

So they ran, turning the tight corners and sprinting down the lengths of the tight, marbled floors as the hedge walls loomed on either side. They passed the rabbit in the maze. He held his paw tight against his red belly as he hobbled down one of the other turns. He cursed them as they passed, baring his needled teeth and glaring with his small, shining eyes.

"The Roses take you!"

But then the Knight and Squire turned, and the rabbit was gone. Soon, even his curses faded away as the ground changed from marble to gravel.

They ran.

They ran and ran and ran.

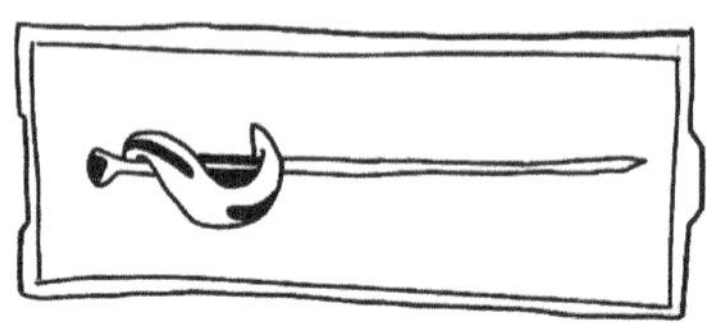

WANDERINGS

T he Moon peeked over the height of the maze wall, sending its frigid light down to mingle with the Knight's smoldering fire. A spark popped, arching to land on his shoulder. He brushed it off with a tired hand and went back to scribbling in the dirt with his knife. They had lost the gravel an hour ago. All the better too, the Knight thought. He didn't want to spread his bed on rocks.

The Squire sat opposite, with his arms wrapped tight around his knees. The boy gazed into the meager pyre of twigs, eyes drifting. He sniffed.

"Master," he said after a time.

The Knight grunted, adding another swirl to the dirt.

"... did the stone warn of the gallery?"

The Knight's brow dropped to the bridge of his nose. "What are you talking about, lad?"

"The stone. The one at the crossway. Was there writ upon it anything of the gallery?"

The Knight grumbled. "Of course there was. As well as the pictogram of the mass of hair. Which would you have preferred? Being drowned in writhing hair, or..." He eased another stroke into the dirt, studied it, then wiped it away with his palm. "It's late, boy. We've another day before us. Best to face it fresh."

But the Squire didn't lay down. He gazed farther into the hall of the maze. Beyond the little circle of their fire, darkness enveloped them like brambles and the walls of the hedge shivered in the wind. Thin streaks of clouds stretched far above, shrouding the Moon.

"Master," the Squire said again. "I mean no disrespect to you. But..." the boy moved his lips like he didn't dare let the words escape, "Can you... really read ancient Purg?"

The Knight was silent. He only stared into the flicker of the fire, ran a knuckle across his peppery jaw.

The Squire said, "There is no shame in it, Master. Even the most learned man finds himself in need of help, at least on occasion."

He leaned to bury his arm in his pack and brought out the bound journal of the blind soldier. The Squire unfolded the saddle blanket from its worn face.

"If we take our time at the next marker-stone and puzzle through it, perhaps we can—"

The Knight snatched the journal from the Squire's hand. His face gone to crimson.

"That old beggar's ravings?" he roared. "I told you to toss this away!"

He waved the book, pages clapping between the bark and leather covers.

"I crossed the desert of Rot with a leg sliced from heel to knee as the sand blasted the skin from my flesh. I ferried priceless Blade-stones over the troll laden waste of the Timber Drop Mountains to the Viziers of the Sleeping King. I served under Kragmael amid the Year Siege and marched upon the Cliffs of Night!"

He tossed the book into the air, and the Squire shielded his face as it crashed into the fire. The flames jumped, curling away the pages greedily.

"I am all we need, boy," the Knight said. "The ancients of Purg made this maze for me to conquer, and conquer it I will! We've two more days till we're finally free of that drunken fool, and I'm not trusting our survival on the ravings of an old fool from that blasted war."

The Knight spat, glaring out into the darkness. "I'm all we need. If that's the worst this place offers, I'd welcome a true trial with open arms. Trust me, lad."

The Squire wished he did. But as the fire cooled to ashes and as the Moon inched overhead, he kept bringing his hand to the pocket at his breast and the scrap of the Rabbit's painting he had hidden.

The Squire woke, hiding his face from the sun and blinking the grit from his eyes. It was nearing midday. He kicked from his blanket and twisted to see the Knight taking long, full breaths with his hands folded upon his chest.

"Master," he said, throat terribly dry. He pulled his canteen from his pack and drank deep, water dribbling down his chin. He patted at the Knight's shoulder. "Master, we've slept the day near to nothing!"

The Knight's eyes fluttered open, weak at first, but the Knight had always been slow to rise and stiff in the mornings. His master sniffed and tweaked his nose, rubbing his mustache.

"I've never slept so deep," he said, something like surprise coloring his voice. "And yet my limbs feel weak as a babe's."

They broke camp, packing their blankets away and shuffling the dusty remains of their fire into the hedges. The Knight breathed deep the air and checked the marks on his gauntlet. "We've surely run most of the maze by now," he said. "I expect we'll find our prize before evening and spend the rest of our time recovering our strength as we work our way back. We shall feast with the Duke and bid a fond farewell to our dear, slobbering Viscount."

And so they marched. The Knight marking their way upon his gauntlet, and the Squire keeping a wary eye on the sun as it shimmered closer and closer to the other side of the maze's high wall. His Master seemed in good cheer, humming a waltz to himself as they plodded along.

As the day before, they never came to a wall. The maze flowed in a continuing swirl, going this way and that; at one point they came to what might have been another colonnade, but the thorny vines and black flowers had taken it over. They had to watch their step or get sliced through the leather of their boots. The Squire was happy to leave the place behind.

And then they came to another Stone.

"Let me teach you reasoning," the Knight said, clapping the boy on the shoulder. "Do you see the marking running up and down the Stone?"

The Squire did. The writing seemed to wriggle, jeering at them.

"I see."

"Do you also see how the drawings on the left have a sharper feel to them?"

They certainly did. The lines and swirls all seemed to attack one another in a towering melee. The Squire pointed to the other column. "You are saying those look the more peaceful of the two?"

"Yes. You seem to be catching on, lad. See how these pictograms look to be flatter, some laying down? I deduce they are in response to these warring ones. And look! Some even appear to have thorns. Remember what the rabbit warned us of, of the Roses?"

"I don't think he warned us of them. Wished upon us, more like."

The Knight waved his hand. "Regardless, they are something to be avoided. And I believe that the column on the right is the least threatening of the two. So, it is right we shall go." The Knight marked the direction on his gauntlet and marched, crunching gravel beneath his heel.

The Squire risked another glance at the stone as they passed. True, he saw the same threatening nature of one column over the other, but what bothered the Squire was how both sides seemed to laugh at them.

A silver gate blocked their way. And no matter how the Knight twisted, he couldn't so much as force a leg through the bars.

"Perhaps I can slink through, master?" the Squire said.

"No, your noggin is larger 'round than a cantaloupe." The Knight crossed his arms and squinted past the shining gate. "I can't see what lies beyond—the hedge turns ahead—but I reason we can climb it. Here, lend me your shoulder."

The Squire did, and the Knight clambered up and over, landing with a clatter of iron as his sword and buckles danced about him. They regarded one another between the bars of the gate.

"How shall I get across?" the Squire asked.

"You are young," the Knight said. "Climb it. But toss your pack over first. No need to haul that."

The Squire shrugged his pack, sent it flying, and gripped the silver of the gate. The bars ran up and down, with none leading across to give him a ladder, but the Knight had spoken true. He was young and pulled himself up.

"Careful of the spikes," the Knight said. "And there seem to be some tendrils from the hedge snaking along the gate's length nearer the top. Don't get snagged by those evil thorns."

"Yes, Master," the Squire said, batting one of the reaching vines from his path. It seemed to quiver and coil when struck, but Squire was sure he had imagined so. A vine cannot move beyond what the wind allows.

He crunched to the gravel path alongside the Knight and shouldered his pack. His Master beamed down at him. "There you are," he said. "There is no obstacle the maze puts forth that we cannot overcome. Now, step to, and take my rapier. I shall wield my broadsword. Whatever lies beyond the turn we shall face armed."

The Squire had often wielded his Master's rapier, so it was no stranger in his grasp, and after their ordeal the day before he found a rare comfort in its weight and fell into step behind the Knight.

He bit into his cheek as they rounded the corner. What would they find? Another colonnade? Those horrible roses the rabbit had cursed upon them? Or would it be another day of aimless walking? Somehow, that thought was worse than any danger that might wait: to wander empty hedgerows till their food turned to molding crumbs. The Squire gripped the rapier with new frustration. To die in battle would be better than to waste away.

Gravel turned to grass. Heavenly soft and thick, like the earth had been blessed with green cotton. As they moved, their footsteps were perfectly masked. Anyone could sneak upon us here, the Squire noted, and cast an eye over his shoulder as the gate turned from view.

They followed the curve.

"Blast it!" the Knight cursed, "This can't be right! This bewitched maze has lead in a circle as round as the moon and yet we have not doubled back on the gate!"

It was true. By the Squire's compass, they should have rounded back long ago.

But they hadn't.

And they didn't.

And they still had not, after an hour.

The Knight whirled around. "I'm heading back!" he said. "We're following the stone to the left, no matter the threat that lays in wait for us. Come along, lad. And keep your arm up, don't let your blade touch the ground. Switch hands if you must, but stay ready."

It was not twenty paces before they came across an impossible clearing.

The hedges fell away like a deep breath. Grass filled the earth, handsomely cut without the faintest hint of thorns. A wide fountain bubbled before them, sparkling in the fading, noon sun. Center of it all, leading with a cobblestone drive, sat a manor house overflowing with windows. Its door loomed large and cherry red, and the brass knocker had been cast in the drooping shape of the earthy flowers they'd seen throughout the maze.

The Knight and Squire stood there a moment. Turning. Taking it in. The boy swallowed an ugly lump in his throat and tipped his sword point for the manor.

"We did not pass this, did we?"

The Knight didn't answer, only clopped his mouth like a fish. His mustache bristled. "This be the work of Wizards, lad! Of corrupting sorcery or some such madness. The Ancients of Purg were a strange folk indeed to build this."

"Do you suppose someone lives here?"

The Knight kicked a tuft of grass. "Someone sees to all this. Though what manner of beast he be, I can not guess. Could be another deviling rabbit or perhaps a fiendish badger."

He dried his hands in the grass and gripped his broadsword anew. "Keep at the ready. Be prepared for anything."

"You mean to go in?"

"Of course I do. We are in need of foodstuffs and I wouldn't mind a stay in a bed tonight."

The Squire's mouth fell. "We will not find the center tonight?"

"Do you see a lovely sign saying so?" the Knight said. "Perhaps an arrow pointing the way? No. And I'm not in favor of staying another night between those hedgerows. Besides, we might find more than just supplies. What if there is a map to be had?"

The Knight walked around the bubbling fountain, up the steps to the manor's red door, and set to pounding the knocker. The bashing sound filled the manor and echoed out into the surrounding yard and the Squire renewed his grip on the rapier, promising not to be surprised at whatever face showed itself when the door opened—man or beast.

The Knight thwacked the brass knocker one last time, letting the clangor fade into the house and took a healthy step from the door, sword at the ready.

They waited.

Crickets and their brethren trilled in the hedges around the edge of the yard. Above them, the sky darkened to a dull red as the sun fell from view. What wind that caught at their clothes felt colored with autumn. The Squire could smell the sea hidden beneath the earthen perfume of the black flowers.

A grumble.

A cough.

Movement from the other side of the door and the creak, stomp, of troubled footsteps. The Squire held his breath as the door sighed opened.

A man peered through. His skin was gaunt and his cheeks were shallow, but his face held the crimson glow of a gardener. His dark eyes flitted between them.

"You're not from the bloody procession are you?" he asked in a high wheeze. "We weren't expecting them till tomorrow. Well into tomorrow, that."

The Knight, frazzled from the lack of bite in the man's voice, opened and shut his mouth trying to catch some words of use. The Gardener dipped his cherry nose toward their swords.

"What're you plan'n with them toad-stickers, eh?" he said.

The Knight looked to his blade as if noticing it for the first time.

"I am a Knight of Norland traveling the maze. I seek shelter for the night. Have you room here?"

The Gardener bobbed his head. "Oh, aye, aye. We've room enough," he said and pulled the door wide, walking with it as he did (it was a large door), "Sorry for snapp'n at ye. Thought you of the lord's parade come early. We've much to prepare yet before he arrives."

They followed him in, his movements old and troubled as if he were a man made from wood instead of flesh. The Knight felt a twinkling recollection as they stepped into the manor, but it darted from him like a firefly on a Summer's night.

The house was built of wood of the deepest grays, like the shine of a doll's eye. Its walls and ceilings swirled with carved moldings and rose high before them. The Squire took his shoes from his feet before treading upon the deep red carpets. The Knight gave his mud no thought and strode after the gardener.

"Run'n the maze are ye?" the thin man asked. "It's been some seasons since I last saw a new soul traveling Purg. A few seasons indeed."

"Are we near the finish?" the Knight asked.

The Gardener shrugged his thin shoulders. "I'm not the one to ask," was all he'd say.

They came into a sitting-room with a tall, crackling fireplace. More folk milled about, tasting little bits of this and that while staring out the wide window into the maze below.

The Gardener lifted a gnarled hand and spoke to the room, "Presenting a bold Knight of Norland and his humble Squire."

The others, the Squire saw, were as sun-colored as the gardener but decidedly plumper. An older gentleman with a trim, white beard and glasses that flashed red from the fire, rose to meet them. His mouth opened into a gapping smile.

"Great Scott, Mr. Lester! Fetch a case of wine and see to Pip for some bread. Go on, shoo! We've not been so honored in years."

He rushed their way as the Gardener scurried for the door. The old man thrust out a gloved hand and pumped the Knight's arm.

"Norland!" he cried. "Its name has been gone from my lips for too long. Norland!" he cried again, a smile splitting his face.

"I am humbled, good sir," the Knight said, "to hear my country so honored."

"Oh, pah," said the old man and leaned to whisper. "You honor us. Tell me, what news of Norland?"

As they spoke, the others in the room drew nearer, and the Squire turned to see more glide in from the halls like bored ghosts. It wasn't long before the room crowded with them, twenty or more, to see the new arrivals to the Manor.

The Squire frowned, worry growing in his gut. Who were these people? Other runners of the maze?

Their old host wrinkled his eyes as he asked, "Please forgive me, my noble guest, but were you one who marched in the Year Siege?"

The Squire watched as his master's smile grew to a ruby glow. He dusted imaginary dust from his chest plate and said, "I served under Kragmael."

The old man's eyes popped from his head and his lips pushed for words, but nothing but a gasp could escape from them. He made to kneel.

"My, lord," he breathed. The Knight beamed down at the man's wispy hair.

The Squire looked on in some amazement as the room responded in kind, taking a knee before his master. It had been some time since they had been so honored. And, in truth, it was hard to receive much in the way of honor with the Viscount bubbling spirits at your side.

The gardener returned lofting a tray of bread and wine as the old man stretched standing again. He thrust his hands into the air.

"A feast, Mr. Lester," he cried, making the gardener jump. "This night we honor our most esteemed guest."

He leaned toward the Knight, a deep hunger in his shining eyes, "Perhaps you could even spare us a tale of your exploits, yes? Hear of the epics of Norland?"

The Knight's smile rose all the more, and he threw his arms wide as if to embrace the room.

"What tales I have recited to kings, I shall impart to you!"

The crowd cheered. Clapping hands and deep-bellied laughs filled the space, and a warmth that rivaled even the fire at the room's head covered the Squire as his master followed the jovial faces deeper in. He moved to follow, but a sharp hand seized his shoulder.

He whirled to see a woman, one of the maids, gazing at him with a painted face and round eyes.

"Oh, mustn't bother the honored guest, little ducky. He's people, after all." and her thin hand smothered his face before he could cry out. He twisted, but her arms were horribly strong. She drug him from the room even as he kicked. He bit into her hand, but the woman didn't even flinch.

"I've got a nice spot for you, little ducky," she said as the crowd's voice lifted into a wild laugh at a joke from the Knight. The Squire could see him, but his face was turned from his. No matter how he squirmed in the maid's grasp, his master took no notice.

They went from the room and into the hall. The noise of their struggle seemed so loud to the Squire. Surely someone might hear him and come to his aid!

Two men happened by dressed in work-clothes and brimmed hats. They nodded toward the busy room.

"Found another one, eh?" one said.

The Squire heard the maid giggle. "And right before the parade too," she said. Her sharp fingers dug deeper into his face. "Just our luck! Give me a hand won't you, I wanna get back to hear the windbag's story before the others sop it up."

The man took his legs and they bore him farther along. The Squire struggled to see where they took him.

It was a dark, heavy door.

Fear flexed in his chest like he'd never known before and he twisted and raged and wept into the maid's hand, begging even as the two who carried him laughed.

The door opened, and the man said, "Do you think Sylvie will make that gravy tonight? The one with the rabbit livers?"

They tossed him in and down.

Down,

Down,

Down,

To the waiting hands below.

STRANGER STILL

The Knight beheld the red, canopied bed; the linen sheets, and goose-down pillows. Across the room, a fire muttered in a wide hearth. The air smelled of warmth. The Knight held his face steady even as his heart swelled. How long since he'd slept on a mattress? How long had he been traversing the wilds of Norland with that sodden oaf of a Viscount?

Too long.

"I trust it is satisfactory?" The old man with the trim beard asked, peeking from the doorframe. The Knight nodded.

"I have made do with far worse, I assure you." He turned to honor his host with a bow. "How can I ever repay your kindness?"

The old man flustered. "You have graced us with your stay here at the Manor—what with your tales of mighty deeds and conquests. We ask nothing else but for you to make yourself feel at home. Rest well, for the King arrives with the morning!"

The Knight paused in shrugging his pack. "In truth?" he asked.

"Yes! The King of Purg honors us. His parade roams the maze and tomorrow it will blast its silver trumpets toward our humble home."

A king! The Knight padded his sleeves, his trousers; finding them grimy. He would have to prepare. For a King is neither Viscount nor Duke. If he could earn his graces... He slapped open his pack to rummage for his best shirt. "Have you seen my Squire?" the Knight asked.

The old man wrinkled his brow. "I do not recall a Squire entering the manor... but surely one as mighty as you does not require a child to babysit like a milk-maid." He leaned closer. "I've never heard tales such as yours, Sir Knight. Your battles. Your quests!"

"Yes," the Knight said.

True, he was no babysitter. If the Boy was off gallivanting across the manor grounds, he'd have a word with him when he returned.

"Shall I share some of my exploits when the Good King of Purg arrives?" the Knight asked. "I've saved my best story for last, you know. I was planning on sharing it with the entire house tomorrow before the boy and I left, but... Well, if it is a king coming to call," he smiled, "I suppose I could prolong my stay a day or so."

The old man grinned and pressed his hands together. "It would be an honor, Sir Knight. May you stay a hundred years. But... I wonder," he leaned farther still, his smiling face seemed carved from wood, "could you share a bit of that story with me? I could fetch some tea and we'd have a lovely evening. Just us."

The Knight laughed and clapped his host on the shoulder, finding it firmer than he'd expect. "You flatter me too much, but I must decline. This is a tale I do not share often, and I find it's best served as a rare vintage."

The old man's smile slipped (but only a moment) and he spread his hands out before him. "Say no more. I shall leave you to rest. Sleep well, noble Knight."

The door clicked shut, and the Knight upended his pack. He found his shirt, but his trousers would need ample scrubbing before they were ready to kneel before a king.

A king! How long had it been since he'd stood before royalty? True royalty, not petty pretenders like the Viscount. He must look his best. The Knight would have to polish his gauntlet, shine his armor; wear his rapier at his hip and broadsword across his back. He surveyed his kit lined across the bed. Where had his rapier gotten to?

"Boy," he called. "I need..." but he was alone. He must have misplaced the Squire while entertaining their hosts, telling them...

He frowned. What had he told them? He knew he had spent hours gripping them with words of his exploits, but...exactly which exploits had those been?

He brought his hand to his face, closed his eyes, but it was like trying to remember a tune lost to years. He felt very cold then, right down to the roots of his hair. "Blast it!" he said. "I'm not an old dotter, for heaven's sake! I told them about... about..." he pulled at his hair. "Snakes and dogs!"

They were gone. He didn't know how or why, but his stories were as lost as if he'd thrown them to a fire and watched the pages curl and crumble.

He clapped his face. Breathed.

"Kragmael. The Sleeping king. The...The Siege year—some of it—I still have those. Perhaps it's this place? If I should step foot from it, would everything come rushing back again?"

He took up his kit, shouldered his pack, and turned for the door. The hinges were well oiled, so he was as silent as smoke as he crept into the dim hallway. He saw no one, and the fine carpet underfoot masked his steps as he padded along.

A silver moon shone through a high window, lighting his way to the hall where he'd shared his stories with the folk of the manor. If he remembered true, the door to the grounds was just off from it. The Knight passed through light and shadow as he glided through moonlight. Then he came to the place and froze.

The room was just as he'd left it, save for the diminished fire in the massive hearth, eaten away to glowing ashes. They had left the curtains rising to the high ceilings drawn to allow the moon to shine through, throwing shadows from the couches and chairs about the room. Nothing had been cleaned. There were still cups and platters and crumbs of food on the tables. But that wasn't the strangest thing...

Everyone was still here, you see.

They sat on the ground, lined before the fireplace with their legs stretched before them like dolls. Each of their faces hung frozen in expression: some jovial, some sad, some coy, some grumbly. Each stared with their unblinking eyes toward the wall.

He saw their host. At first, he thought the man stared straight for him, but as the Knight crossed the carpet, the man's eyes failed to follow.

Were they dead? None looked to be breathing. After pulling a deep breath himself, the Knight crossed into the room, careful of every step. As he came upon them, that old nagging feeling returned—the hint of recollection. Then the Knight clapped a hand to his mouth as his eyes forced ever wider.

"Punch!" he gasped. "Punch! They're just like those horrid puppets!"

And it was true. As he stood over them, he saw their painted faces; their carved brows and chins. Some wore gloves, but not all. Some had hands so exquisitely carved they rivaled even the finest of sculptures. He knelt before the puppet of the old man with the trimmed beard. So detailed and finely painted was his face that Knight thought surely this couldn't be! Then he struck a knuckle against the puppet's nose and heard the hollow tap.

He had spoken to this puppet. Seen him speak back. It smiled, and laughed, and puzzled, and wrinkled its brow; could a puppet carved from wood do all that?

And where were the puppeteers?

The Knight straightened. Stepped back from the horrible line of wooden figures and tightened his fist around the sword at his hip. He circled his head to the rest of the room. Was he truly alone? The moonlight gave little cheer to the place, and the Knight didn't like the way the shadows seemed to smile. He left there, feeling a dancing chill as he turned his back to the smiling puppets.

He faced the front door. They'd barred it with an oak brace as wide as his shoulders and chained it shut.

He wet his lips. Scratched the stubble at his chin. Their hosts seemed to have locked them in for the night. He glared at the brace, his brow wrinkling into heavy lines.

"A Knight of Norland is not so easily bested!" he hissed and lifted his arm to strike—but then a smell arose around him, as if some beast had filled the Manor with its breath. He stayed his hand, blade held aloft as he sniffed.

"It's those bloody flowers from the maze!" he said, spinning to face the hall. At its end, he spied a dark door. It lulled open an inch like a sleepy eye. The Knight could feel a draft against his face and with it, the scent of those cursed flowers.

He set towards it, crossing the doorway to the puppets' sitting room and turned a wary eye to the lifeless line at the fireplace. He expected one of them to blink. To turn its head his way and shout an alarm, but all stared perfectly ahead.

He walked the length of the hall and stood before the dark door. The smell was like a fat hand pressing into his face, smothering him. He draped an arm over his nose and wedged the way through with the flat of his sword.

He saw coats. He brought his sword to use again, peeking past to see farther in.

More coats, all hanging by their drooping mouths as far as the moonlight allowed. It was perfect darkness beyond (the Knight could not see even a hint of the closet's end) and wafting forth like breath was the earthy scent of dark flowers.

The Knight shouldered his way in. Dust coated his arms and shoulders. The door was far behind him and soon what light allowed only gave the hint of the shapes before him.

Then the way angled down.

The coats were soon over his head. His hair brushed the hems, and rivulets of dust rained upon him in the dark. He turned to see the crack of light from the door. He had not gone far, but already it seemed leagues away. The Knight batted at the coats overhead.

"I feel like a child!" he said.

Down he marched, sword held ready and ears straining for the smallest of sounds. At last, he heard a struggle from the deep dark.

He braced himself and strengthened his arm. Should some beast come at him in the dark, he'd split it to ribbons before it brought a fang or blade upon him.

Light ahead: the shallow strip of a candle leaking through a door in the near darkness. He padded closer, blinking at the change. A sad door hung before him and groaned as he pushed through. He heard a voice cry out from within.

"Don't come closer, you monsters!"

The Knight stood at the door's mouth. Inside was a room with a bare dirt floor lit by a dribbling candle. In its center was the Squire, hanging with ropes looped around his legs. His face was pale and his eyes red, but his smile glowed at the Knight's approach.

"Master," he said. "Oh, thank God. Thank God!"

"It's alright, boy. Keep your voice." The Knight rushed to lift him and brought his sword to the ropes. The Squire wrapped his arms around the Knight's legs and wept bitterly.

"They took me away," he said. "Dragged me down here and tied me up. They pinched me like I was a pig waiting to roast!"

"Don't worry, lad," the Knight said, turning to see the dim room. Another door led deeper in, looking sadder than the first. He pulled the Squire to his feet. "We're leaving."

"They said a parade was coming," the Squire said, "but I don't think it's one with candy and ribbons."

"I doubt so, boy. Those puppets mean to do us some mischief. We need to leave here before—"

But the Knight's words died on his lips. Behind them, they heard the distant creak of a door and the rustle of coats. The Squire's eyes went wide, and the Knight spun to face the sloping path leading back up into the manor.

At first, all he saw was darkness, an inky black like the space between stars, but then the form of a man. He walked with a stiff motion and slapping feet. As he came toward them, the Knight heard his voice.

"Noble Knight!" their bearded host said. "You seem to have wandered from your room. I do hope you are not lost."

The wooden man came to a stop just beyond the door. His brow wrinkled impossibly over his carved nose. "You were not planning of leaving, were you? So soon? You promised a story, remember?" The puppet lurched a step, then another. "Let me guide you back to your room. You will want to be rested when the King arrives. He loves a show and you've the makings of a great one."

The Knight cut his head off. The smiling face clunked to the stone floor like a bucket.

"Run!" The Knight cried.

The Squire pointed up the way to the wardrobe like a drowning man. "But the way out—"

"Do you want to be a puppet? Fly, boy. Fly!"

They ran into the dark, away from the creature.

Before the light left them, the Knight gazed back. The puppet stood, hands clasped politely before him, with his wooden skull rocking like a dropped toy at his feet. From his headless shoulders rose a face dripping with eyes and pinchers. It pulled itself up through the puppet's hollow neck with the blade-like legs of a spider, impossibly large for the body it inhabited.

They ran far in the dark with their arms spread out before them, brushing into the rough walls as they stumbled on and on. It was not long before the Knight could hear their pursuers, even over the huff of his pulling breath. The Squire spoke up, wasting air.

"Puppets don't move on their own, master," he said. "What drives them on?"

The Knight wanted to smack his head, but couldn't see it in the dark. He was too busy sucking air into his burning chest to answer. He only gasped, demanding more speed.

He prayed what he had seen had never been. He prayed the horror scuttling after them was nothing but a horrid dream.

And then their arms folded into a rough door that shuddered open, spilling light into their starving eyes. They slammed it shut again with a crash and braced their shoulders against it. The Knight shook, drawing back his air in great heaves, all the while straining against the spindly wood of the door for a blow that would be sure to come.

And come it did.

The monsters at the other side rushed the door, making the Knight click his teeth and bite the side of his tongue. He heard the death-song of a thousand splinters spreading their hands over the door like the crackle of a spine.

"A toast!" said a voice from beyond, "A toast to the brave Knight!"

"Open to us, we shall feast."

"We shall feast together!"

"We've a lovely drink for you."

"Yes! YES! Change you to something else!"

Voice after jeering voice called from beyond the door, pressing and shaking it as the Knight's strength leaked away.

"Master!" his Squire called. He twisted an eye to see the boy rushing his way with a brace. They forced it into the iron bars of the door and stumbled away, watching the door bounce and buckle.

The Knight fell to his knees, feeling his stomach climb higher and higher into his throat as he fought for breath. "That won't... hold long...."

The Squire paced the floor before him, hands pulling through his hair as he spun to see the room. The walls were nothing but carved earth and sloppy, to boot. A furnace lay cold and forgotten with a hill of coal skirting its legs and staining the room black as smoke. For weapons, they had only the Knight's broad-sword and the coal for throwing.

No way out.

The Knight hung his head, tongue lulled and bleeding from his mouth. "Dead end," he said. "At last. We found our dead end."

The door rumbled its agreement, and the Squire scrambled up the pile of coal. The boy tried to open the heavy iron of the furnace, but its hinges were red and fading away from rust. He beat his fists against it. "Oh, to die in this cupboard!" the Squire cried. "Why did you burn the old man's book? Why didn't you see the trap for what it was?" He fell back into the coals, sending them pebbling down, and buried his head in his arms, shoulders shaking. "Why," he moaned. "Why did we ever come to this place?"

The Knight had no answer. He looked at the faded marks of chalk on his gauntlet. They'd taken one too many turns. No tracing their way back now.

The door shuddered and the creatures beyond laughed.

"I... I'm sorry, boy," the Knight said. "I forgot it was a maze. I was... so eager..." but the Knight had no words. He could only shake his head and spit blood into the coal-black dirt.

But then light flickered in the Squire's eyes. He pulled his face from his arms and spun to see the room.

"Master," he said. "This is a coal cellar."

"Aye, it is. There are worse places to meet your end. But there are far better."

"No, not our end!" The Squire kicked his heels into the rattling pile and sent a wave of the stuff to the floor. "This came from somewhere."

The Knight's eyes jumped. He stood straight and bent his neck to squint into the dark ceiling, but the Squire had already spotted it.

"A chute!" he said. "We can climb out. It's not a dead-end!"

The Knight studied the square slit above the coal heap. Cobwebs hung from it like inky veils. Could they even reach it? The Knight scrambled up alongside the Squire. He stretched his arms, clawed his fingers into the rough wall; kicked and scratched with the toes of his boots. He caught nothing but the wisp of cleaner air drifting from above.

A seam the width of a nail crunched over the door's face. A dark claw wiggled and gouged to push through. The door arched like a cat.

"Lend me your shoulder, boy," the Knight said. "Perhaps I'll yet reach it."

The Squire pulled his face from the sight of the buckling door. "My shoulder?"

"Yes! Here, press your back against the wall. Don't bend. I'll need a good purchase to lift up and out."

The Squire backed away, sending more coal scuttling across the floor. "But how will I get out?"

The Knight sputtered. "What's that to mean? You'll hold fast to my legs, nitwit! I'll pull us both up. "

The Squire took another step back, gazing up at the chute with a white face. "You'll pull me up?"

"Of course I will! I'm a Knight of Norland! I've hefted boulders thrice your size across the foothills of the Timberdrop."

"That was a long time ago, master."

"BLAST IT ALL!" The Knight shouted. The color of his face had dropped to deeper reds and his hands had turned to grabbing claws. He waved toward the crumbling door. "DO YOU WANT TO BE AN EMPTY HUSK? I will not die here. I will not be one of their puppets and dance in their farces!"

So the Squire braced his arms on the wall as the Knight climbed. His fingers found the chute and gripped its walls. The Knight heaved, his arms shook, and the Squire hung from his ankles like an iron weight. The Knight stretched his lips across his teeth, sucking his breath as sweat drew lines down his neck.

They tumbled together down the coal heap, skinning their hands on the rough floor.

The door jumped. Great gashes opened in its face and the stabbing arm of a beetle pulled through, swiping at the air. The Knight could see its eyes; small, dark, and wet with an evil shine.

The Knight turned his face toward his Squire. The boy's face pale at what he saw through the door. The beetle's sharp face seemed to smile, and it called out in a sharp voice.

"Come closer, little ducky. The king arrives soon. He shall be hungry when he does!"

The Knight pulled to his feet. "Climb atop my shoulders, boy," he said. "We'll have another go."

"But how will you—"

The Knight didn't let the boy finish. He took him by the arm and hurried him back up the shifting coal heap.

The door twisted. Its boards peeled like the bark of a tree, as so many dark claws tried in vain to shiver through.

The Knight heaved the boy. He felt no heavier than a bundle of sticks. "Reach!" he called up. "Climb!"

Then the Squire was gone from his shoulders. The Knight looked up to see the boy's legs dangling from the chute, wriggling further in like a toad to mud.

The Knight drew his sword and spat to the door. "You wanted tales of might?"

All those shining eyes from the splintering door shook with glee. The wood squealed as they pushed through. The iron bar bracing the door shot from its place as the wood turned to dust around it.

"I am the Last Knight of Norland!"

He dove for the door as the beetles stretched their claws to embrace him.

PUPPET DREAMS

The Squire climbed.

Below, he heard only the crash of steel and the roar of the Knight. Around him, only the noise of his breath and the running of his heart like blood in his ears. Frozen lines of sweat brought shivers to his arms. More than once he slipped in the tiny space, only to kick out his knees to wedge himself in. His palms burned, and every breath was like a cloud of ice in his chest.

It was so dark.

As he scrambled up the chute, he prayed for the Knight... That his sword would not fail him. But as the moments died, the sounds of chaos below turned from roars to screams of rage. Then a new sound joined the Squire in the chute. The clicking of claws.

The Squire wasn't alone.

He raced. Scuffing his knuckles raw and scraping his knees and spine in the tiny space. He smelled sky above, but below came a draft of earthy musk and the click-clack-click of claws. Then a voice spoken through teeth.

"Where are you going, little ducky?"

The Squire couldn't even turn to look. He crawled till his head struck the heavy iron of a hinged door. He heard a renewed scratching beneath him.

"We've so much to prepare for the King's arrival! You can't leave yet," the creature called.

The Squire braced his knees in the chute and pushed at the door, flattening his face against it. He could taste dust in his mouth, feel the crunch in his teeth.

"Silly, ducky." The climbing thing was at his heels. He could feel its bobbing feelers at his ankles. "None can escape the King of Purg. Only surrender to him."

The hatch swung up, cracking like a splintering bar. The Squire's hands found the coal chute's sides and scrambled out. Above, the moon shone bright, full and deathly cold upon the Manor. The earthen smell had gone, and the grass was soft and kind under the Squire's hands. Then he dug his fingers into the lawn's tufts and found a stone.

Behind him, the thing leaked from the mouth of the chute like a roach inching from the rotten wood of a log. Its body was long, with wet scales that twinkled in the moonlight. Its dark eyes found his. It hissed like a kettle.

"Why don't you come back inside, little ducky?"

He threw the stone, striking the creature in the center of its sharp, smiling face.

The thing shrieked, legs scratching like chalk on the sides of the chute. Its face dripped with something black, and the earthen smell returned.

"The Roses take you!" the creature cursed.

The Squire found another stone.

And another.

And another.

As he pelted it, the beetle hissed and spat and cursed, but it didn't slither any farther from the chute. In fact, the Squire suspected it was stuck. The hatch leading out had been tight.

The Squire left it there, running away with great, heaving breaths. The monster screamed, something about the King of Purg. Or roses. Or some other nonsense; the Squire didn't care. His bare feet dug into the cold lawn. He could feel the dirty tug of spider-webs as he ran between the skinny trees along the side of the house.

Then he faced the Manor's sealed door.

His hair hung in a wet mop before his eyes, his arms and legs trembled with little jolts, and he struggled to keep his breath in his chest like it was an animal writhing to get away.

I should leave, a voice spoke up within him. I should leave this vile place and not look back. My master chose this to be his final folly. Let him have it.

But another voice—and this one quieter still—if you left him... where would you go?

He found one last stone hiding in the dewy manor grounds and circled till he found a window. The Squire used the rock as a hammer, working fast in case the monsters heard the racket, then vaulted over and through.

He dropped into the sitting room with the crunch of glass underfoot. He saw the puppets first. They sat before the fire-place and the Squire had half a mind to toss them onto the hearth and find some matches, especially when he saw the maid's painted face lifeless among them. What sort of place was this?

The Squire wandered from the room, careful to keep from the windows' glow. He paused before every door and strained to listen. He peeked into every hall, a hair at a time.

He found a smoking room with more dust than carpet, a bed-chamber whose only occupants were the spiders lurking in the high corners, and so many cupboards and closets and washrooms that he wondered how the Manor could have possibly held them all. The whole while the Squire followed his nose, searching for that earthen scent.

Then at last he came to a parlor bigger than all the others put together. Like much of the house, the room was a deep crimson with sinking carpets. High chandeliers hung unlit above and (unlike most of the Manor) the Squire did not spy a mote of dust. They had kept this room clean. So much so that a small part of his mind chided him for setting foot in the place.

Each wall held a portrait, all the same man dressed in fine robes. In one he posed before a dead boar, as massive as any creature from legend—yet still—the man looked somehow larger. In another, he held a sword aloft with a peaceful face; legions of decapitated foes at his feet. And here he sat beside a beautiful woman as scores besides looked on with dripping envy. And then another—somehow the worst of all—of the man in profile, kneeling to give a young girl an ornate pitcher. Her face was one of apprehension and her fingers looked to shake as she reached for it. The man's smile looked cruel.

The Squire circled. A little lower on the wall was another, this just of his face, looking into the parlor with a benign expression. What captured the Squire's attention, however, was the man's eyes. In each portrait, while his face kept calm, his eyes were cold. Furious.

They were the most terrifying eyes the Squire had ever seen.

Could this be the king of Purg? he wondered, and took the little portrait from the wall.

Whoever had painted this had also done many for the Rabbit's Gallery, he realized, and reached into this pocket.

The scrap of the Rabbit's prized work coiled at his touch like a snake, but the Squire pressed his lips and got hold of it. He turned the portrait away, drew the wriggling remnants of the vile painting from his pocket, and slapped it where he imagined the king's nose might have been.

The change was immediate.

The frame shook, feeling shockingly warm in his grasp. He nearly dropped it. Then, after a few more stutters and burps, the painting stilled. The Squire stretched his arms far from his body, like the thing in his grasp was a dead body rather than a picture.

He imagined the hypnotized faces of the souls trapped in the Rabbit's Gallery. Would it work on monsters as well as it worked on people? The Squire didn't know, but he felt better to at least have something to use against these beetles other than stones.

He looked at the largest painting, stretching almost the whole of the room. The King of Purg sat astride a horse, looking out upon the Garden Maze with a look of merry boredom. In his hand, he held the ornate pitcher. This was the only painting without the man looking down into the room, so his eyes looked... not kind—they were too cold for that—but more... accomplished? And there was something in the way his fingers clung to the pitcher, as if glued.

The Squire turned from the room, all its paintings, and sulked again into the hall. The pale moon still shone in the windows, unmoving, and the shadows he shimmered through held a thick chill.

The smell of those dark flowers grew with every breath.

He passed silent doors, each one tall and dark, then at last the Squire froze. He turned his ear to hear.

A struggle. Not far, a few doors down perhaps: the sound of a man kicking at walls.

The Squire padded faster, painting tucked under his arm. Another crash and a muffled curse lead him to the last door in the hall. Its wood was dark as the sky behind the moon.

Again, that little voice came. Sneered. Told him to leave the bumbling knight to his fate.

Then the other voice, quieter still.

He opened the door.

The Knight lay stretched on a hewn table. Beetles with spiny limbs and mean, squinted faces stood at either end as he struggled. They glared with shining eyes, twitching and working their jaws. One beetle stood apart from the others. His dark shell glistened with dew. On his back, he hauled a bulging satchel of the black flowers from the maze. The Squire's eyes burned at the smell.

One by one, the beetles' heads snapped toward the Squire at the door. The Knight's eyes found his. He raised his brow and grumbled beneath the gag his captors had fixed between his teeth.

"Oh good. We don't have to go looking for you after all."

From behind the table, their host paced into view. He held his smiling head cradled in his arms. His voice hissed out from the hollow hole in his neck. "The Knight went through such pains to see you out," he said. "I was just telling him how wasteful that had been. Here, what do you think?"

The wooden man pulled the gag from the Knight's mouth.

The Squire watched as his master doubled over and gagged, dark matter falling from his lips. The Knight gathered his breath and glared at the walking puppet with fevered eyes. He rose weak on his arms.

He said, "Blasted worm! Face me fair and I'll—"

He gagged as they stuffed the waxy leaves into his mouth. The Knight squirmed, trying to spit the mash away, but they held his mouth shut and plugged his nose.

The Squire gripped the frame under his arm.

"Free him," he said.

The host shrugged his headless shoulders. "We needed some fresh faces here," he said. "We fear the King has been growing bored with the usual show, but with a knight in the company!" He laughed, the sound bubbling up from his chest. "We've had to make do with common folk and their common stories for so long. Now we shall have tales of heroics. The King shall be pleased!"

The Squire's stomach riled. He could taste the sweat on his lips and feel its sting on his eyes. The beetles marched from the Knight, twisting on the table, and turned their bobbing feelers his way.

He pulled the painting from under his arm and held it over his head.

Every eye in the room flicked up to see it. For a horrible moment, the Squire feared it hadn't worked, that those sharp hands would tear him to so many pieces like paper tossed to the air. But then the beetle's heads lulled. Their cutting jaws jittered and dripped like a rotting feast unfurled before them.

The Knight freed his mouth from their grip. Bloodless scratches covered his face, and he rolled to spit and vomit the earthy leaves. He shuddered, lifting himself from the table. His hair hung before his face like a curtain and his shoulders shook as he coughed soundlessly.

The Squire didn't see their host with his head in his arms move from his place. A curved knife flashed in the puppet's hand and plunged into the Knight's side. His master's face opened in shock and he wrestled against the puppet as it loomed over him.

The empty head clattered to the ground as the puppet brought his arm down upon the Knight's face. The old knight's teeth clicked like the slam of a door and he slumped to the ground. Unmoving.

The puppet stood over the Knight, the only sound a dead whir leaking from its hollow chest. It rolled its shoulders. Clicked a foot on the ground.

"I'm angry now," the thing said. "Can't make a puppet of a corpse."

Its headless body shook as if a chill had filled it like a cup. Its hands opened and closed.

"But I've learned to use what I have. The show must go on, and all that. Tell me, Squire," it spun to march, arms quivering at its sides, "what stories do you have?"

The painting hung useless in his hands. He backed from the room, but his heel caught the door's lip and he wobbled to the floor. The Puppet strode after.

"You'll take his place, little fool. You should have fled into the maze." The puppet's hands trembled with fury. "You don't need your eyes to be a puppet, you know."

The Squire swallowed a scream. Held the painting over his face. Shut his eyes.

Then a crunch sounded from the room, the crack of a table breaking its back against the wall, brought the Squire back again from behind the frame.

The Knight stood in place of the puppet. His hair hung in gray strings from his skull. His spine bobbed like a reed in the wind and the knife in his side was like a red horn. He brought a shaking hand to his face.

"I'm in a bad sort, boy."

His voice rattled like wind rushing over a jar and his breath was like the wheeze of a pipe-organ.

The squire set the painting aside, propping it on the wall. "Still yourself, master," he said.

The Knight pressed a stiff hand against the Squire's shoulder, and the boy took his weight. In the room beyond, he saw their host's splintered body, broken against the table. A furious quiver of dark antenna came from the ruin, but it dared not crawl forth.

"The Roses take you!" the creature cursed. "You and your precious Norland! You and your countrymen!"

The Knight shook the hair from his face and his eyes crossed the room like a man woken from deepest slumber. The Squire saw his face twitch; saw the pain dancing beneath his skin. When he took the man's hand in his own, it wasn't skin he felt: only the smooth polish of fine wood.

The Knight's eyes met his. They were painted so detailed and fine, from afar you'd swear they held life. When he pulled the knife from his side, no gore spilled to the floor; only a puff of sawdust and a scatter of splinters.

"You didn't eat it all!" The creature called. "The King of Purg shall catch you! He'll chop you for firewood!"

The Knight stood straighter and looked at the painting on the ground with a frown.

"It was so beautiful before," he said. "But it's just a moldy rag spread across some leer's face."

The Squire still dared not look. He tugged at the Knight's arm. "Master, please, let us leave this place. This house turns my stomach to rot."

From his ruined place among the drooling beetles, their host screamed curse after curse. He promised pain; he swore blood, and he begged. It begged and pleaded and screamed terror.

The King comes tomorrow.

The King comes tomorrow.

The Squire helped his master from the room and the door clicked shut behind him.

Even when the manor was far from view, gone from sight behind the walls of the maze, they still heard the shrill cry of the creature's raging.

TIPPING POINT

I t was as the sun rose, that the Knight began to understand in full what had happened. The chill that had taken root in his bones did not leave him. He could feel it *move*, retreating deeper. He looked to his squire. The boy looked hollow. Dark circles clung to his eyes and he walked like a man haunted. He made to set his hand on his shoulder, but he couldn't get his fingers to cooperate. The boy shrugged him away.

"What do we do now?" he asked.

What indeed. The Knight had marched into this place feeling as tall as one of the mighty men who had kept at Kragmael's side, but after the ordeal in the gallery and the horrors those puppets had played on them...

He lifted his offending hand into the rays of the sun. Exquisitely carved, the work of a *master*. He knew he should feel dread at the sight, but as the sun climbed higher and higher overhead, his sense of horror began to melt away and *new* feelings came to replace it.

Fire looked vicious. The dirt beneath his feet was cool and welcoming. Every cloud that passed before the face of the sun woke a fear in his soul, only lifting when the light returned to bathe his sight. He placed a hand over his chest and felt the thud of his heart and the lift and fall of his lungs as he took breath.

I am a man.

I am a puppet.

The two battled in his mind like warriors in a blood-sport. He feared whoever won…he'd lose. For without a soul, a puppet is just wood for the fire, and without flesh his being would *dart* like a bird free of its cage. For now, both wrestled, and the Knight lived. But he knew he couldn't wobble between the two forever. Eventually, he would fall.

And then what?

"Perhaps we could follow the turns on your gauntlet?" the Squire said, pulling the knight from his grim reverie. The sun was overhead now.

The boy said, "Or maybe we could *cut* our way out? We still have one sword. We could put it to good use."

The Knight's mind turned slow, and at last, he said, "I fear the notes written upon my gauntlet are of little use in this place, nor do I believe bringing up our fist against the maze shall bode well. I'm sorry boy. I have been bested." The Knight hated the words even as he spoke them, but they were true. The Maze had conquered him.

"But you've faced trials greater than *this*," the Squire pleaded.

The Knight hadn't the strength to behold the Squire's face. There was fear in his voice; *anger* as well. To have failed so completely was agony enough, but to have fallen so far in the eyes of the boy? This was almost more than the Knight could bear. He strained to close his hand (carved so fine, yet so utterly *useless)* and turned his eye to the perfect blue of the sky. The part of him carved from wood *drank* the warmth like a beast parched of thirst, and the part that was still himself frowned with confusion at the dark shape dropping through the air.

The dark shaft of an arrow sprouted from his chest, sounding with a hollow *THUNK*.

A strange sight—the Knight's first thought—*to see a barbed shaft wobbling from your wishbone.* He regarded it the same you would horsefly. His second thought was given to the fellow exploding from the hedge.

His dark, navy vest had been stained from days of pursuit. Gone was his suit and tails, and gone was his high smile and haughty eyes. His long ears laid back on his skull and his white, hanging teeth flashed as he readied another shaft.

"Visited the puppet show, did you? I trust you left it in *shambles* like you did my beautiful gallery!"

The second arrow landed solidly into the Knight's arm. Already the Rabbit had another pulled and ready to fly. He aimed for the Squire.

"I've rubbed the arrowheads in *seeping ivy,*" he said. "A *scratch* would see the boy turn to a puddle on the ground, too weak to even scream."

The Squire squared his shoulders to rush him, but a look from the Rabbit froze him where he stood. Warm air drifted overhead, sending the dark petals shimmering down from above. Before, the flower's scent had been numbing, but now the smell sharpened the Knight's painted eyes.

"What do you want?" the Knight asked.

The Rabbit gave a wicked smile. "Perhaps I just want to see both of you dead on the ground?"

"You've had your chance at that."

"*He still does,*" the Squire whispered.

The Rabbit's eyes flashed. "To be fair, I *was* on my way to cut your eyes from your heads, but then I saw the lovely hell you unleashed on those poor, unsuspecting creatures. They've proved themselves *rude* to many of mine over the years, you see."

"Can't imagine why."

The Rabbit's eyes narrowed at the Squire. "I *was* going to kill you, but then I had a *better* idea. You traipsed in here after *treasures*, yes?"

The Knight narrowed his eyes. "Of a sort," he said. "Though, truly, we would just as soon bid this maze farewell."

"Oh, *you really mean to?*" the Rabbit laughed, "You and everybody else in this bloody maze. Only, it's not really a maze, *is it?*"

The Squire's brow furrowed. "It isn't? Then what—"

"Have you ever been to the Sea, boy?" the Rabbit crooned. "Ever walked the piers over the turning waters and seen the old fishermen with their frostbitten faces—too aged for open ocean—drawing up, hand over hand, their frayed ropes from the icy depths? *They* know what this place is. They would behold it with watery eyes and *curse* it even as they sang its praises."

"Stay thy tongue, lest you cut your teeth," the Knight said. "You love your own voice *far* too much for my ears. What is it you want?"

The Rabbit stared a moment. The Knight thought he could see his mind working behind his creased eyes. His pink tongue flashed over his lips. "My desire is the twin of yours," he said. "This place has trapped me the same as anyone else. And once the King discovers my beautiful gallery is no more..." he shrugged his shoulders. "Unlike most in this place, my mind has *not* addled away. My ears have remained faithful and vigilant since the beginning and I've heard *much*."

"So you know the way out?" the Squire asked, a fragile hope in his voice.

The Rabbit smiled. "*A* way, boy. And it will not be easy." He waved toward the Squire, "I require a resourceful and unassuming youth...and," he let fly another arrow at the Knight, this one coming to a violent, humming stop at his throat, "a *brave Knight*, who has recently become very *difficult* to kill."

The Knight plucked the arrow from his neck, sawdust coloring his doublet. While it was true he no longer feared blade nor beast; the memory of the Knight he had been was fast fading away.

"What is it you desire of us?" he asked.

"There is one man who holds sway of the Garden Maze. The means for our escape lay with him."

The Squire's eyes lit with recognition. "The King of Purg."

Rabbit's smile twisted grim. "Aye, the *Last* King of Purg. The last of Purg *itself*! This King and his Maze are all that remain of that ancient folk, outliving all the rest."

"But Purg vanished into legend and wives-tales *eons* ago," the Knight said. "Surely this be not the *same* king!"

"*You* want to tell me of this place? Go on, I'll sit awhile and listen. Perhaps you can tell me of the Baker's house and his ovens, or of the laughing man and his children?" The rabbit leaned close, his eyes twin fires. "There are places here where air turns to *glass* and men's bones claw to escape their own *flesh*." He slung his bow over his shoulder. Straightened his vest. "Bless your fortune to have only come across the *puppet show*."

The cold pit grew larger in the Knight's belly. His wooden frame, so unyielding, wanted to seize and spread roots where he stood. He could *hear* the music in the soil calling and the sweet drink of the sun lulling him into that warm dark.

Then his Squire's hand was at his arm. "*Master?*"

He forced his eyes to blink, an audible click in his ears, and willed his neck to bend and behold the boy's face. Days of hard travel had dulled his features and the dust in his hair made him look older than his days.

Fear in his eyes.

Curse these limbs! He forced his arms to bend and his legs to kneel with a noise like the popping branches. He looked into the Rabbit's eye.

"You will guide us past these horrors?"

"I certainly won't give *tours*."

"And in exchange, we're to help you against this enemy?"

"So you *were* listening. Yes. Join me to face the king, and you'll take leave of this place still holding tight to your little lives." He extended his paw. "A bargain?"

The Knight stretched his hand to shake. "You'll see us out?"

The Rabbit winked. "I can promise the boy shall once again breathe free air and that you, Noble Knight, shall never dance in one of the King's puppet shows."

The Squire came between them. "I don't understand," he said, "you say the King is the *last* of Purg."

"That he is. Everyone else are poor fools like yourselves who've wandered in."

"But how has he *lived* all this time? Where did everyone else go?"

"Oh dear, child," the Rabbit said. "The King is of the *old* world; a magician. He *ate* them."

KING'S PARADE

T he Squire pricked his thumb on a thorn as he climbed
the waxy hedge. The aroma of the drooping black flowers was strong here, and the sharp calls of the rabbit down
below did nothing to help his grip.

"Shimmy left!" the Rabbit said. "The vines don't weave as
thick there."

The Knight, who stayed cross-armed at the Rabbit's side,
watched the Squire climb with a squinted, splintery brow. His
beard, once alive and vigorous, was now a smooth, paled grey.
He brought his hand to his face, fingers stiff and slow, and
called up. "Those vines are alive, boy," he said. "Grip them
gentle and they'll treat you same."

The Squire grunted as he pulled his foot free from the
hedge, sending the wide and shiny leaves fluttering down.
Every hold seemed to close as he came to it, like the Maze

was teasing him. He dug his elbow into another tangle of vines, ignoring the thorns drawing white lines on his skin, and pulled up.

Nearly to the top.

"I thought you knew the way," the Squire called down.

"Clean your ears, boy!" The Rabbit stood in the crook of the Knight's arm. "I said I knew a way out! Now hustle to the top and tell me if you spy any pennants."

Pennants? It brought back to mind the Century Fair and the Duke and their wager, lost by several days now. The rabbit had led them deeper and deeper into the hedge maze, guiding them past perils and berating them as they went. Rarely an hour passed that didn't see the rabbit scratching at their pride in some little way. The little creature seemed to grow stronger at every dirty look the Squire sent his way, so he took effort in ignoring him.

It surprised him to see the Knight remain unfazed by the creature's constant belittling as he marched on, stiffly and quietly (more often than not with the little beast perched on his shoulder). Rarely did his master's carved face leave the sky.

When the Squire, at last, crested the crown of the hedge and felt the blast of wind kiss his face... for a moment, he could pretend he was out. That he was safe.

He had once seen the vast fields of red grain from the balustrades of the Old Tower; the ocean from the Dickinson Docks, which stretched nearly a mile into the open sea on twiggy stilts; he'd looked out upon the great expanse of Norland from the Timberdrop Mountains, and watched as the sun set upon it, as the stars opened their eyes one by one. The Squire had seen many places during his travels with the Knight, but none could compare to the Maze of Purg.

Endless. Slopping up until the maze became the far lips of a bowl. Waxy green as far as the Squire could spy. It was a vast country of turning paths. So many were the patterns and designs that, for a moment, the Squire thought it beautiful. He stretched his neck to see the sky. It was a blue deeper than blue without even the thought of a cloud. The air baked around him—rippling—but the rush of wind blasting his hair from his face did much to cool him.

The Rabbit crooned from below. "Look for pennants! Red pennants!"

He scanned the view, looking for red among the green.

And then he saw them, blinking into view like a magic trick. Pennants—thousands of them—peeking up and over the distant hedges. More and more rose into view.

Then the ground shook, and the Squire had to hold fast to the hedge, lest he go tumbling down. Below, the Knight rode out the quake on wobbly legs as the Rabbit grabbed tighter at his arm, eyes wide.

"How far out is it?" he said. "How far?"

The Squire turned to see, searching again for...

The pennants were even higher than before, and more were climbing to join them. They rose high. And the hedges...

The Squire had to squint.

The hedges were... moving; curling and uncurling like vines. A ripple rushed through the maze, like someone had lobbed a stone into a green pond.

"The King's Parade!" the Rabbit cried, "How close IS it, fool?"

The Squire's hedge shook. In the distance, he could hear the roar of countless waxy leaves moving, moving. Coming closer.

"The maze!" the Squire said. "It's changing!"

"Climb down!" the Rabbit cried, "Climb down! Climb—"

The Rabbit let out an oof as the Knight dropped him into the dusty gravel underfoot. He forced up his arms and stretched his fingers.

"Jump, lad, I'll catch you!"

The Squire peered down. His master looked like a wooden toy with his brittle arms raised toward heaven. If he let go of the hedge, the Knight would just snap like so many twigs. He scanned the vines under his feet, looking for a path down.

"I think I can make it!" he said.

"Jump, fool!" The rabbit said, "The maze will crush you."

But the Knight had become weaker by the day—by the hour, it sometimes seemed. Even opening and closing his hands looked to be a chore for him. No, he didn't trust his master to catch him.

"Haste, boy!" The Knight cried as the Squire took his first few wobbling steps down. He looked for holds in the vines, spaces for his foot, and loops in the leaves for his hands. In his rush, he found many thorns and his fingers became sticky with blood.

And then it was too late.

A great tremor passed through the hedge, like a ghost slipping into a corpse. The leaves rattled. Thorns quaked. Vines wound around his limbs.

"Jump, boy!" the Knight cried again, but the roar of the maze swallowed his voice, like a storm at sea.

The hedge bent, tipping forward like a domino, and it was all the Squire could do to hang on as the earth rushed to meet him.

Thorns bit into his palms and the thunder of the maze collapsing surrounded him. Then the vines drew him in deeper still, pulling at him like so many ropes until the green swallowed him whole.

Leaves filled his face. They crunched in his ears and squeezed his arms to his sides as the Squire fought for breath.

Then the earth shook, and all was still.

The wall ejected him onto pebbled ground as the Squire kicked his way free of the thorns. He scrambled away from the leaves until his shaking arms could no longer hold him. The Squire let his face come to rest against the gravel, its pattern pressing into the flesh of his cheek.

The flap of a pennant sounded from high above, but he couldn't be bothered to find it with his eye. His arms and legs burned with a myriad of cuts, and his hands felt hot and shaky. He risked a peek, unfurling his fingers.

The palm shone red, stained with blood, and the wounds lashed into his flesh were many. The air burned, so he let his fist shut once more.

He needed to find the others, but his eyes drifted shut once more.

So tired.

The blast of a horn, distant and shrill, poked into his ears like fingers. He opened his eyes.

The maze had changed. What was once an endless, curving hall had transformed into a wide-open space, like the horrid manor from so many days ago. Where the gravel ended, trim grass began. The Squire could smell it: a sweet aroma that reminded him of happy summer evenings chasing fireflies.

Then he spied beyond and blinked in surprise. Tents of all shapes and colors filled his view. At first, he thought some miracle had occurred, and he'd returned once more to the Century Fair, but that happy fantasy couldn't remain for long.

No one would confuse what the Squire saw now with so human a thing as the Century Fair.

It was a city of canvas. Tents rose from the ground that were larger than some towns he'd visited with the Knight in their travels. There were even towers that stretched high into the air, with balconies and windows and flags clapping in the breeze.

And there was a breeze. For the first time in weeks, the air in the maze moved, and the Squire breathed a sigh of heavenly relief as he pulled fresh air into his lungs. It smelled of roses.

He had to find the others.

The wall of the maze seemed to shiver as the Squire neared it. Its thorns looked like teeth, eager to tear. The leaves were too thick to see anything beyond.

"Master," he called, loud as he dared. "Are you there?"

He heard a cough from the other side. "Boy?" the Knight said. "Are you well? Nothing broken?"

The Squire patted down his arms with the backs of his hands, shaking loose what leaves still clung to him. "I think I'm alright," he said.

"What color are the flowers on your side?" This was the Rabbit. He coughed, like he'd tried to swallow a mouth of dust. "Do you see roses?"

"No," the Squire said. "There are no flowers at all."

"Oh, thank God," the Rabbit sighed. "And the King's Parade, do you see that?"

"The tents?"

"Yes, all the daft, bloody tents. Do you see them?!"

He did. In the time he'd had his back turned, the number had nearly doubled. "What should I do?" he asked.

Silence from the other side.

"We shall find a way through," the Knight said. "Is there anyone about? More of those horrid puppets?"

The Squire didn't know. The sun was setting. Colored lights dotted the tents in the distance.

"Avoid anyone you may come across," the Rabbit said after another fit of coughing. "Don't trust your eyes. Even a smile can hide the sharpest of teeth. Find somewhere to hide and wait for us."

The Squire entered an empty city of whispering tents. And though amber lights hung on stout poles, the way kept strangely dark and the stars overhead were stark and cold. Wind buffeted at his back.

He strained to hear any sign of life: the dim mutter of voices or the busyness of whoever had set up these massive tents. Strange light seemed to shine from within them, a wet and inky light that hurt the Squire's teeth to look at—like he was hearing them rather than seeing them.

Strange happenings, he thought. How far would the Knight and Rabbit have to march to find their way in? And where, in all of this strangeness, would the Squire hide? The wind cut brutally between the towers and the hum of the pennants brought an ill feeling to his soul.

This is a haunted place.

His wandering legs came to a stop near one tent, this one darker and less sickly than the others. Its canvas, colored like a star-field, sparkled in the dim light of the lanterns. The tent was open and a glowing mist filled the space, yet he couldn't see within.

He strained his eyes, inching closer. There was movement in the mist, like oil curling through water. A small face appeared in the fog, with empty eyes darker than the ocean at midnight.

The Squire started back, losing his footing and landing soundly on his rear. Gravel from the path bit into the cuts in his hands. The face in the mist smiled, and the mouth formed silent words.

Do you see me?

The Squire ran, spraying gravel underfoot. He lost track of where he was going. It didn't matter where he ended up, just as long as it was somewhere far away.

He fell, clutching at his chest and gasping for air. The night sky above him blurred. He tasted metal on his tongue and smelled the blood on his hands, and rose shakily to his knees. He couldn't see the wall of the hedge maze anymore. The brightly colored tents swallowed the view and were so large and overlapping, it was difficult to discern where one ended and another began.

"Another maze," the Squire said, screwing his eyes shut to it all. How was he to find the Knight now? His lungs burned too much to care right then and he willed himself to stand, hand at his throat.

He heard the fountain then.

It was tall but not wide; built like an obsidian tower in a circle of soft grass. At its peak, a statue of the king gazed into the far distance. Water bubbled at his feet and the words "DRINK AND BE FILLED" were inscribed in blockish letters.

The water shone in the starlight, its song like the pure chorus of a choir. He inched closer. He could feel the cold sparkle of the fountain as he drew near.

When was the last time he'd had a drink? A day? Longer? The fountain's mist kissed his face as his hands came to rest on the carved stone. The Squire gazed down into his rippling reflection.

Then, before he knew what has happening, the water rushed to meet him and the world tipped end over end. He found himself in the water, the chill of it shocking.

He clawed his way out from the fountain. His clothing heavy—nearly pulling him under once more—and his eyes burned like someone had pressed their thumbs into his sockets. He stretched his leg up and over, sloshing out onto the parade grounds, coughing and gagging into the grass.

What had happened? He patted at a stinging burn on his chin and his hand came away bloody. He must have scrapped the bottom of the fountain, but he couldn't remember diving in...

A hand gripped his shoulder.

"Catch your death like that, son."

The Squire bolted from the man. His voice was deep and graveled, like the folk of the Northern Plains, stretching out their words until they were flat.

He ran right into a woman pushing along her apple cart. Were the Squire a little older, he might have hurt her—but even then, maybe not. Her face was a flat, sunburned-red and her small eyes blinked in surprise. "Beg your pardon, lad!"

(beg'ah paw-den, lawd)

"Best watch your walk'n, there. I'm known ta kick!"

One of her apples toppled from the stack, bounced off the grassy turf, and wobbled to a stop at the Squire's foot. The woman's brow creased, wrinkles rolling into view one after another. She held out her hand.

"Be a friend

(uh fray-ann)

and hand that up, eh?"

He was gone before her wide hand could make a snatch at him. Dashing past her apple cart as the man behind dove after. He heard the racket of the cart getting tossed aside and the angry howl of the woman.

Breathless, he ran. The shouts of the man and woman became distant as his heart shook in his chest.

The din of a thousand voices filled the surrounding air. The tents, once glowing and hidden, were open and clapping in the summer wind as folk moved about within. Worst of all was the burning circle of the sun, hanging high in the crystal blue sky.

He found the Parade's edge and ducked behind a squat tent. Someone had stacked a collection of barrels in the place, so he squirmed away from view. Hiding among the sun-baked wood, he clutched at his knees and collected his breath.

By the Sleeping King, what happened? Had he hit his head? He pressed his palms into his eyes till he saw sparks. Trust nothing, the Rabbit had said... Was this a trick? One giant ruse of the Garden? He tried to block it all out, to will the sky to return to night, but the noise of the parade was like a chain wrapped around his head.

Find a place to hide. Wait for the others.

A horn sounded like the sharp cry of a wolf, and the Squire inched out to see.

A little distance from the grounds, the wall of the Garden Maze stood like the rampart of a keep. As he watched, the hedge shivered, and a procession emerged like frogs pushing through pond scum. The men wore a signet of gold upon their breast and walked in lines of two. Boots of heavy leather sank into the sod at their coming, and they covered their faces with deep masks of silver. With strong iron poles over their shoulders, they carried cages.

In one, a man dressed in soiled finery sat with an empty gaze. Another held what looked to be a bear, its dark fur muddied and its wet eyes looking out. A pale woman clutched at the bars of her cage. Tears dripped from her chin as she wept, eyes darting between the guards—too scared to make a sound.

The man at their head brought a shining horn to the lips of his mask and let out another mournful cry. Then he spoke in a screaming shout, "GUESTS OF BLESSED ONE, HE OF PURG'S EYE; WELCOME TO BLOOD AND RUIN. "

The man in the silver mask marched like a general before the cages. He kicked up sod with the sharp points of his boots at every step.

"THE KING IN HIS MERCY HAS DECLARED YOUR LIVES BE LIFTED IN NOBLE DEATH. AND IN PUNISH-MENT FOR YOUR TRESPASS INTO HIS SANCTUARY, YOUR END SHALL NOT BE FINAL; BUT STUNTED. IN HIS DEEP MERCY, A SECOND CHANCE SHALL BE OFFERED TO THOSE OF YOU WHO PROVE WORTHY."

The man in the cage stared ahead, unblinking. The woman pressed her mouth against her fingers, gripping at the bars as she shook and the bear let out a keening cry.

The Squire couldn't watch.

Had these people come from the Century Fair? The woman might have been one of the Northern folk. He'd seen a few during the Viscount's assault of the booze dens, but the man could have been from anywhere. He didn't know what to think of the bear.

"PURG'S EYE SEES YOU!"

The Squire jumped like a bat had dived at his neck. Had he discovered him? He whirled, nearly toppling over the barrels, expecting to see that shining mask staring down at him. All he saw was blue sky.

The men answered their commander. "PURG'S EYE SEES ME!"

They were moving; hefting the cages over their shoulders and marching into the parade. The Squire thought they looked like the great oxen he'd seen in the desert, with their wide shoulders rippling with muscle. From where he hid, he could smell them. He risked a look as they marched by. There might have been thirty men, he wasn't sure—and more cages than the ones he'd seen. Many more.

They couldn't have all come from the Century Fair. This many people going missing to never return? Folk would go looking for them, surely.

They carried the cages deeper into the Parade, into the throng of tents.

The Squire's heart pulled at his throat. How were the Knight and Rabbit going to make their way through all of this—and all the way to the King, besides? He strained to see the tops of the surrounding tents, impossibly large. How long would it take them to find this person? A day? Longer?

He peeked past the barrel. He could still see the tail end of the procession as they hauled their prisoners.

They were on their way to the King, right? Perhaps he could follow? He bit his lip, heart hammering as the last silver mask stomped down the path and out of sight. The Squire darted from safety and half crouching, half running; he followed.

Tailing them proved easier than expected. It seemed most folk were happy avoiding the King's enforcers. The guards never looked back and the people they carried were too busy in their misery to notice the boy creeping after, sticking to the shadows. He could see inside the tents now, he realized—whether that was because of his dip in the fountain, he couldn't say—but now when he risked glimpses into the tent folds, no haze blocked his view.

Strange things he saw. Odd things. Nothing overtly frightening, but everything he dared to view left him with smothering unease.

One was a bakery. He knew it by the heavenly smell, but when he glanced inside, he saw only a dog chained to the ground, unmoving.

Another tent held... people he supposed. He could not see them, but he heard them speaking to one another, as if in a debate. The language was a harsh one, the sort that made the word 'Flower' sound like something that might sneak in during the night to cut you.

The tents grew in size as they traveled deeper, like this place was an old forest thick with trees.

One tent held a library that rose in a spiral, each book with a blood-red eye on its spine. In another, they had formed a chopping block from stone. It sat among a flood of white flowers and the perfume wafting out nearly drew the Squire inside.

The worst tent he did not dare to look within. It had turned the earth surrounding to slush and a horrid wet, snapping sound echoed from inside.

The parade felt to be both crowded and empty, to where the Squire felt as if he was sneaking through a city of ghosts. The way was long and twisting, seemingly devoid of rea-son—at least from where he stood.

At last, they came to a wide tent as gray as a thunder-head. The guards carried their burdens inside and they left the Squire alone in the Parade. As he stirred, waiting for the courage to follow, people of all sorts drifted out from the tents. Their faces were strained, and they eyed the wide, gray tent with a tired weariness. One such man, dressed simply with a mop of coarse, white hair upon his head, hauled a sack of what looked to be melons. He strode out onto the gravel road. The man muttered to himself. "Not my fault, I lied... not my fault..."

The Squire held his breath as he passed. His smell was like milk left to crust in the sun. When the man's voice faded into the distance, the Squire threw himself onto the path and hurried for the gray tent. Other people were about, yes, but he prayed they were like him in not wanting attention.

Ducking headlong through the open tent-flap would be suicide. Instead, the Squire traced along the tent's front and ducked into an alley. More barrels, though these sloshed with something foul as he scampered over. Hidden from the street, the Squire waited for his heart to slow, pulling breath after slow breath.

He listened, expecting the clop of heavy boots or the piggish snort of the man in the silver mask. But nothing came. Perhaps his luck was at last on the mend.

He lifted the heavy canvas and rolled under into the dark.

The air felt heavy and hot on his face. Wet like the bogs that pooled at the roots of the Timberdrop. Goblin country. With some hesitation, the Squire took his first breath in the gray tent.

Heat shimmered in his nostrils like fumes. The smell was of too many unwashed bodies and all the filth that came with it. Dots of sweat covered his face and stung his eyes. The cuts in his arms and hands had their say as well.

If he had to venture a guess, he would have said the tent was a storage place. Crates and more of those tepid barrels stacked high into the air, forming its own messy corridor he found himself in. The space was dark, but the hazy light of a lantern leaked up and over the boxes.

The Squire wiped at his brow with an arm. How could anyone stand it in here? He felt like he was suffocating.

The booming voice of the herald made him jump. He couldn't make out the words, but they were quick and angry.

Then he heard the soldiers leaving.

This is foolish, he thought as he crept along the stack of sweltering crates, foolish and dangerous.

A sob broke through the musty dark and another shushed it with a hiss. He could hear the heavy pant of an animal and smell its musk the closer he came. When he, at last, slunk out into the open space beyond, the sight confounded him.

A sunken pit encompassed nearly the whole of the tent. An apparatus of some sort hung over like a twisted chandelier. Cages hung from it on chains. Some sat high in the air and some lower down in the dark of the pit. Each held a forlorn soul. There were too many to count.

He saw the bear first. Its eyes rolled madly in its skull while its dark tongue lulled from its jaws. Slime dribbled from its mouth, stretching down to the other cages in the pit. The cage nearest to the ground belonged to the woman he had seen. She didn't react to the line of drool from the bear above. Her bruised face remained blank, staring into nothing.

The Squire shook his head. What had these people done to have earned a fate such as this? He paced closer, the smell of the space overwhelming him. Give aid, as the Knight would say. It is the very duty of a steward of the Sleeping King. Such is our oath. The Squire had never taken an oath, nor had he sworn to any man, save for the Knight.

And look where that got me.

The woman's eyes flickered to life. Her face found the Squire's form in the dark. "You," she said, and pressed closer to the bars, pointing with a shaking finger. "... a boy? Only a boy?"

His throat hurt to speak. "What... What is this place?"

He saw the shine of her eyes in the lantern light. "You know this place. You're... You're standing in it."

He looked to his feet. Coarse sand surrounded the pit. He said, "I'm sorry, I don't understand."

"Do you still have a name?" her voice broke as she sobbed into her arm. "A name? Do you still have a name, boy?"

The question shook him. Of course, he had a name. Everyone had a name. His fingers curled... nails biting into the cuts in his palm. He has a name. A good name. His mother had called him... His mother... She used to carry him on her back through the grain fields. The sun was always red and beautiful as it set.

Remember the wolves? Running through the dark...

her body shielding yours...

The Squire blinked away the memory, and the woman coughed, dry and violent.

"Will you help me?" she said. "I've been here months, but together we can find the path out again!"

The Squire felt weak, like he'd taken a blow to the head. He wobbled where he stood. "A way... out?"

"Yes, yes!" the woman lifted her arm high as she could and pointed to the domed roof of her prison. "The latch is there. Please, I cannot reach... the bars cut."

It was a simple device. Hardly a lock. All it asked was to be turned up and out.

Wait for us, the Rabbit had said, hide and wait for us. But the woman's eyes pleaded.

"I've heard there is a tree," she said, "with fruit of gold that grants your deepest wishes. If we find it, we can escape from this place. We can find our names again!"

The Squire's mouth was horribly dry. A hot line of saliva drizzled from above, dotting his shoulder. A mournful rumble from the bear filled the tent. The Squire could feel it in his gut.

He stepped for the cage. "What about all the others?" he said, stretching to reach the latch. "When my friends get here, maybe we can—"

She seized hold of his arm and screamed. "HERE! HERE! By the bloody eye, PLEEEEEASE!"

The Squire couldn't twist away, so he sunk his teeth into her wrist. She cursed him, her grip failing only slightly, but it was enough. He slipped his arm free as she wailed.

"THE ROSES TAKE YOU, DEVIL!" she screamed, spittle dripping from her chin. "Curse you! CURSE YOU!"

The others in the cages came to sudden life, blinking as if roused from a dark sleep by the woman's shouts. Hundreds of eyes turned toward the Squire, and so many hands reached out in desperation; some pleading, some wailing, some cursing, like the woman. The very air in the tent vibrated with their anguish.

The Squire stared, open-mouthed. Surely not all of them had come from the Century Fair. Something dark stirred in his mind. It repeated the woman's words.

I've been here months. But how could that be?

He spun, ready to charge back to the hiding place behind the crates, but the shadow of a man stood just behind him. The Squire stared up into the wink of a silver mask in the lamp-light.

A DREADFUL AUDIENCE

T he man had small hands and led the Squire through the Parade with a pinching grip. Whenever someone was unfortunate enough to get in their way, he lashed out with a booming shout, "*BUSINESS OF THE KING! STAND ASIDE!*" He was very loud in the Squire's ear.

Hide! the rabbit had said. *Hide and wait for us!*

He strained to glimpse the sun as it winked between the pennants high above. How long until they realize he'd been caught?

The Herald shook him. "MIND YOUR GAZE!" he said in a loud whine. His mouth stretched under his silver mask. He had teeth the color of smoke. *"THE KING HAS TAKEN EYES FOR LESS. ONLY LOOK UPON HIM IF HE DEMANDS."*

The Squire nodded. This seemed to appease the Herald, and he clapped his shoulder. "I was like you once," he said, the first words he had not shouted to the heavens. "The King is a fair man. He will give you a good death and a better life afterward."

The Squire lost his footing a moment, and the Herald hefted him right again. *"Steady, boy!"* some of the annoyance creeping back into his voice. *"I'm doing you a good deed."*

The Herald cut through an ally and into a congested street. Folk mulling about and looking busy, appeared as fake as the puppets from the manor. They were still flesh and blood, the Squire thought, but it was like they were playing a part in a drama. A portly man with a powdered face and colored doublet hurried past. Another gentleman in a frumpy hat followed, repeating some rhyme like an exercise.

"Thumbs in the daylight,

"Fall from great height...", over and over.

The Herald leaned to say, "The King honors diligence. Remember that."

They arrived at the King's tent. The Squire shook when he saw it. It was a *Palace*. A *Castle*. A *Monument* of which he'd never seen the equal in all of his travels with the Knight (at least of those he could still remember).

The sunlight danced—actually *danced*—on the crimson canvas. He wasn't even certain it *was* canvas; it could have been spun from the silk of the clouds and dyed red with the blood of *Saints*! Turrets rose, spearing the sky with their peeks and flags (so many of them!) thundered like the roaring of an army. Embroidered over all of it were roses.

Thousands upon *thousands* of roses.

A knock to the head broke the Squire from his staring. *"Look at nothing,"* the Herald hissed. *"Keep your gaze on your miserable feet."*

He did as told.

Two orc-men stood guard at the tent's entrance. They wore silver masks, the same as the others, and their green eyes shone out like emeralds. They smelled like moss.

"BUSINESS OF THE KING!" the Herald said, back to his screechy self.

The shine of their silver masks stared back at them. The orc-men stood aside, one of them mumbling, "For the honor of Purg's Eye."

They walked inside. The Squire kept his eyes on the ground.

The soft grass vanished in favor of white marble tiles, very much like what he had seen in the Rabbit's gallery. But *unlike* the gallery, he spied flecks of gold in the marble. Gentle music, like a breeze in a meadow, drifted overhead.

And then his voice, bidding them stop.

The Squire had stood in the presence of many powerful men in his time with the Knight: Kings and Warlords, Bishops and Dark Ones, Generals and Wisemen—none could have frozen the air with a word.

"No," he said.

Everything froze. The music, the click of the Herald's heel, even the glint of the tile floor held its breath. The Squire realized he was shaking.

In the quiet, he heard the man stand, the fabric of his robes moving and then the soft *slap* of bare feet. The Squire kept his eyes on the ground.

"Explain this," the man said.

The Herald wasted no time. "This one snuck into the guest's enclosure," he said.

"And you caught him?"

"No. One of our new arrivals. A woman."

"Bring her," the King said.

"Right away."

"And leave this one."

The Herald's hand vanished from his shoulder, and the man's hasty retreat echoed. After silence returned, it was several moments before the King spoke again.

"Who sent you?" he asked. "Duchess, Duke, or Child?"

The Squire was unsure of the question, but then remembered the wide smile of the Duke and the dark wager he had made with them. He'd been so happy guiding them to the maze.

The Squire spoke, his mouth dry and sticking. "It was the Duke. He... calls himself the Duke of Purg."

The King's laughter was like sunlight. "He *does*, then? Well, we shall talk next time I see him. *Odd* for him to invest his efforts in the likes of *you*. It is usually the Duchess who gathers the younger souls, what with her doe eyes and kind smile. Was there anyone else who came into my sanctuary with you?"

The Squire kept his eyes on his own feet. He worked his mouth. "No one else. Only I."

Silence for a moment.

"Only you..."

The King took hold of the Squire's chin with his thumb and forefinger. Slowly, he tilted his head till they stared eye to eye.

He was the same man he had seen from the paintings in the manor. His face looked chiseled, boasting a firm chin and strong eyes. *Overpowering* eyes. They sparkled gray and violent. He wore a thick robe of crimson and—like his palace—countless roses embroidered its surface. The robe was the work of a craftsman beyond anything the Squire had ever seen.

The room surrounding was like the finest museum. Hulking tapestries hung from overhead, many of them acting as dividing curtains for rooms farther in. The light of the sun filled the space to perfection and the subtle movement of the tent's great walls kept the air cool.

A modest orchestra waited in silence on the far side of the room and standing next to the King of Purg's throne (a high-reaching monolith, cut from the darkest onyx) was a girl holding tight to an ornate pitcher.

The Squire's breath caught when he saw her. He'd seen her before, from one of the paintings in that horrible manor. She wore the same haunted face and stared only at the ground.

"Look at *me*," the King said.

The Squire had no choice but to obey. The King's eyes held him captive, same as chains of iron.

"Speak it again," he said. "Just once more. Did you come alone?"

The Click of heels sounded through the room and the Herald came forth. His smile stretched under his silver mask, grey teeth on display. "Here she is, my King. Fetched prompt—"

"*NO*," the King roared. The Squire shuddered like as if struck. The King's voice was more terrible than a thunder strike. He returned his gaze to the boy, the picture of calm.

"Tell me," he said.

The Squire wet his lips. "... I came with my master."

"Ah?" The King's brow rose. "And where is *he?*"

"The maze separated us. I do not know where he is."

It was the truth, albeit only part of it. He knew if the King asked any further, he'd tell *everything*. But the man only stared.

"Captain," the King said.

The Squire heard the crisp *slap!* of a boot and an arm folding to salute.

"Is that the woman?"

"It is, my Lord."

"Let her come forward."

The King released the Squire and turned his attention to the woman from the cage. In the light, the Squire saw her clearly. Her bruised face trembled as the herald forced her forward, step by step. The dress she wore might have been beautiful once, but now it stood as witness to the struggles she'd faced. The King, in his fine robe, peered down at her with a critical eye.

"Who sent you?" he asked. "Duchess, Duke, or Child?"

She choked deep in her throat and dropped to her face before him. "Mercy I cry, my King! I would live to be your servant, cleaning your chambers or tending— "

"*No,*" that stern voice. "Tell me. Duchess... Duke..." he knelt to tip her face up from the floor. "*... or child?*"

Her mouth shook in a tight line. "A child," she sobbed. "He was all alone and reminded me so much of Rubin... he told me—"

"He told you his father had vanished into the maze. That he was a wealthy man—a *widower*—and would reward you, *yes?*"

The *face* she made. It turned the Squire's heart.

"I *am* selfish," she said. "I won't lie. But I would have helped him even if his father was old and penniless. *I would have!*"

"Like you helped this one?" The King tilted his head toward the Squire. "You would betray him for your own freedom?"

The Woman couldn't look at him. Tears streamed down her face. "*... I did...* "

The King cupped her face in his strong hand. "Do not *fret,*" he said, his voice soft and kind. "It is not wrong to seek your own safety. You have proven your fear of me in this and you shall behold your reward."

A tapestry moved behind the King and a servant stepped forth. He wore no mask and his drooping face regarded the King of Purg with a nod.

"My King," he said.

"Lead her to Mr. Bradford. Tell him she is a precious guest."

The servant approached and offered a slender hand to the woman. "With me, please," he said.

The woman left, her face drifting between empty shock and sorrow. Her eyes met the Squire's for the briefest moment. He saw guilt there, horror as well, because she knew if given the chance... she would betray him again. It was like a knife in her soul.

She followed the servant out.

The King smiled. "I treasure sacrifice," he said. "To sacrifice one's own virtues is the sweetest of all. Everyone believes themselves so *very* strong and good, until everything falls to dross. Then all they have left *is* their virtue; *that* cannot be stolen away. It must be *given*."

He gave the Squire a sidelong glance as the smile drifted away, tic by tic. "But you have not come to offer a *gift*, have you? No, you are a *thief*."

The Squire backed away. "I've taken *nothing*."

"Haven't you?"

Movement again from the edge of the room and another servant stepped forth. In his hands, he carried the head of a puppet. He offered it to the King.

The King said, "Do you recognize this one?"

The Squire looked into the dead eyes of their host from the manor, his carved face lifeless and still.

"... he was at the manor," the Squire said, a sick feeling growing in his stomach.

"He was indeed. Very good." He tapped at the empty skull with a knuckle. "The creature who once lived in this husk, do you know what he told me? The most interesting thing... a boy and an old man *burned down* that beautiful house of mine. You could *taste* the ashes in the air a league away."

A fire? They had set nothing ablaze, even if they would have *liked* to!

The King beheld the shock on the Squire's face. He laughed and said. "Oh, don't worry. I could sift out the lies from the truth. Neither you *nor* your master started any fire. You *did*, however, drive my poor, innocent puppets to such an end... This is a slight I cannot overlook."

He let the head fall from his hand. It *clunked* onto the marble and rolled, settling to rest at the toe of the Squire's boot.

"I loved the dramas they would dance," the King said. "Can *you* dance?"

The Squire felt like he was one of the beast tamers, with his head laying in the mouth of a lion. He could feel the hand of death resting on his shoulder.

"*Please*," he blurted out. "Let us leave this place. We'll never return—never speak of what we have seen. I give my word! I swear on—"

"On *what*?" the King thundered. "By *what* could you possibly swear on? *Do you know where you stand?* You have *nothing*, boy. You are *dirt*; fowl air drifting within a *trash heap*!"

He towered over the Squire—eyes flashing murder, teeth bared like a wolf. "You are *chaff* for the fire, only worth burning to get *rid* of, and you... S*tole. From. Me.*"

Those three words echoed in the Squire's skull. *This is it. He's about to order my death.* There wasn't anything he could do... nothing left to say.

The King crossed his arms, and a smile played at the edge of his lips. "But despite all those truths, I still wonder: on *what* do you swear?"

This was a test.

Or a trick.

Whatever it was... the Squire withered inside. He'd never been clever (if he was, maybe he wouldn't have ended up in this place). What could he hope to say? *I swear on the King? On the sun and moon? Himself?* There must have been a riddle somewhere that he had missed. He stared back at the floor, at the sparks of gold in the marble, and wished he could just... *disappear*, like in the stories.

"I... I don't swear," he said.

Interest colored the King's voice. "*Oh?* Tell me why."

Sweat drizzled at the nape of his neck. The Squire took a breath. Looked the king in the face. "You're going to kill me no matter what I say. What point is there in making promises? I'm not sorry we ruined your *horrible* puppet show. I'd do it again if I had the chance."

He waited for the blow to come, sword or fist or worse, but it never did. The King only stared, his eyes in slits.

"Good," he said and turned his back to the boy to stride for his throne. The girl holding the pitcher stood straighter as he approached.

The King said, "Take him to the Mirrim. If he lives, he is to be rewarded, but allow him a little time to freshen up first. He looks like he fell from a dung heap."

Then he waved his hand, and the orchestra played once more.

MIRRIM

The Squire faced a mirror. The boy who stared back was not one he knew. He was filthy from his spotted face to his dusty boots. A bruise of deep purple sunk into the side of his neck and continued down beneath his collar. Bags hung beneath his eyes.

Look where trusting that fool Knight got you.

He rubbed the grit from his face with the back of his hand and caught sight of the cuts in his palm and arm. They stood out, bright and angry against his sunburned skin. He squinted to the sun.

Still hasn't moved. Not since he fell into that fountain.

The bucket of clear water they'd given him sparkled and was oh so *cool* on his sorry hide. He soaked a washcloth and rang it out over his head, smiling at the rush of cold water.

The masked man who'd led him to the little enclave in the King's tent waited outside the ornate curtain behind him. He cleared his throat and spoke in a gruff voice. "Don't have all *day*, young sir."

The Squire scowled. He would argue that was *all* they had in this miserable place. He took his time in scrubbing out his hair and letting the water run over his face and arms.

When he at last stepped past the curtain, expecting the gruff hand of the guard to attach to his neck like a bat, he blinked in surprise when the silver masked man was nowhere to be seen. The girl stood outside, holding tight to her heavy pitcher. Her pinched face stared at the ground.

"*Do'yah* still have a name?" she asked, speaking the words a little too quickly.

The Squire frowned, thinking she was poking fun. "Do you?" he asked.

"Yes. But only because the King knows I don't like it."

"What is it?"

"I told you, I don't *like it.*"

Her mouth scrunched to one side—a nervous habit—and her eyes darted to his face and away again. "He's not *all* bad," she said. "Well, *he is*, but... sometimes he makes it snow."

"Snow?"

Her mouth flattened into a frown. "... that's what I said, right? You get snow where you come from?"

"I... wandered around a lot." The Squire shook his head. "Are you... What happened to the guard?"

"Talus had to go. King wanted him. I'm going to take you to the Mirrim." She shifted her grip on the pitcher and tipped her head farther down the path. "We should hurry. You'll have a better chance if we hurry."

She spun to leave, careful not to spill a drop from the pitcher she carried. The Squire followed.

He eyed the heavy load. "Would you like me to—"

"No. I don't. You can, um... I'm sorry. What were you going to ask?"

He opened and closed his mouth, loss for words. "... I was going to ask if I could carry that for you."

"That's what I thought. And *no*, not unless you want to keep it."

"Why are you carrying it?"

"What?"

"I said, why are you carrying that pitcher?"

She stopped to look at him. Shook her head. "It's not a pitcher. It's a *cup*."

He studied her face, looking for the joke. She frowned and said, "A pitcher is for holding flowers and being *looked at*. A cup is for drinking. And this is a cup."

The Squire had talked to his share of invalids during his travels with the Knight. He knew the look; knew the manic *absence* in their eyes... this girl, while she certainly *felt* unhinged, didn't quite smell it.

She frowned again. "You're staring at me."

"Oh. I'm sorry, I'll—"

"Just don't fall behind. It's better to be early for the Mirrim."

The Squire had to hurry after.

Like the silver masked guards before, the people of the King's Parade seemed to give the girl her space. Many of them ducked into the various tents that bordered the path as she came by, and some of them looked at her with something close to horror.

A woman saw them coming down the path and such a look of despair came over her. She threw herself to the ground, saying "*Mercy on this old heart, mercy I beg!*"

The girl stepped past, careful not to tread on an arm. "Not today, Madeline," she said. "Perhaps another day."

The Squire jumped to avoid the woman as she spat at them. Curses followed as they continued down the path.

"People are crazy here," the girl holding the pitcher said.

"She's not going to..." the Squire tossed up his arms. "*Chase after us*, or..."

Then the girl looked at him like *he* was crazy. "We're going to the *Mirrim*. They'll leave us alone."

"What is the Mirrim?"

"A *maze*. What else would it be? Just another flavor of the maze."

"You're not telling me on *purpose*."

"You noticed that?"

The Squire stopped. *What was he doing?* The girl walked a few feet more before she noticed. She looked back; her face strained. "We really should—"

"Why don't I just *run?* Why am I following you? This place is meant to kill me, right?"

She held out a hand, the other propping the pitcher on her hip. "It's meant to *test* you. You've made it *this far*, right? Especially if we're early, you can—"

"No." He took a step back. There was an alley a quick dash away. She couldn't chase after *and* hold on to that pitcher.

"This is madness," he said. "*You're* insane. I'm not following you."

She opened her mouth to answer, but the words died on her tongue. She snorted, angry. "*Oh*, I hate these stupid games... okay look, I don't know how things work wherever *you're* from, but we got these things called Pinky Promises. You heard of those? If you can just—"

The Squire darted for the alley, each crunch of gravel underfoot loud as the crash of waves on a ship's kneel. He'd find the Knight and Rabbit, and—

Thorns erupted around his ankles, digging into his skin and sending him headlong into the ground.

"*Hold on, alright?!*" the girl shouted.

Everything stopped. The tendrils from the ground held fast, holding him inches away from a nasty hello with the ground. Thorny vines of the maze weaved around his ankles. He risked turning his head. The girl frowned down at him.

"*Look,*" she said. "I can't *talk* about the Mirrim. Part of the test or something. But what I can do is *this.*" She offered her pinky. "I've never seen anybody talk to the King like you did. So if I help you in there... will you help me too?"

The Squire looked at the vines, frozen and waiting for the word to throttle the life out of him. He looked at the girl. She tried to smile, but she had trouble looking natural at it.

The Squire shook his head but, like it or not, *what choice did he have?*

It was a tent. Of *course*, it was a tent. It rose high in the air and reflected the blue sky like it had been plated with fish scales. Heat shimmered over top of it.

"The Mirrim?" he asked.

The girl nodded. "Once you go in, you'll only have a little time before the others arrive."

"What others?"

"The Mirrim is a... *contest.*" She scanned the grounds, "But if you're *early,* you won't have to deal with any of that."

"Why?"

"Because getting through—" she hissed through her teeth and stumbled, nearly losing her grip on the pitcher. She lifted her foot to find a long spine sticking up out of the ground. It slurped away into the earth almost as soon as they saw it. She growled, kneeling to rub at her foot. "*I wasn't going to say anything!*" she said.

The Squire jumped away, eyes scanning the grass. "*What was that?*"

"*Nothing.* The maze thought I was about to say something I shouldn't." She nodded toward the shimmering tent. "You should head in."

He faced the Mirrim. He couldn't run away, he couldn't learn anything about it beforehand, and he knew above all else that he *couldn't go in there.* It was insanity! *Reward him if he survives,* the King had said. He doubted that meant freedom... just a better form of slavery.

"You mentioned you'd help," he said.

She nodded. "I can't speak about it. Just trust me."

Trust her. He almost laughed. His whole life he'd trusted only one man—blindly trusted. He knew better now.

The Squire padded through the grass toward the tent.

"My name is Missy," the girl called after.

He looked back. "What?"

She shrugged, eyes scanning the sky. "I said my name is Missy. I never liked it."

"Alright."

"I bet your name was Bruce or Gus or some other dumb farmer's name."

"I'm a squire."

"A squire for who?"

The question poked at the bit of his brain he couldn't recall. He's served the Knight his whole life—he knew that—yet many of the memories of that time were... hazy. Only a few images remained, like the ghosts of lantern lights in the dark; the Desert of Rot, the Sky Plains, the Timberdrop Mountains and the Goblins beneath... he knew the places but not the lives they'd lived in them. How had he served under his master?

Did their deeds bring about aid or harm? Could he even call him *master* anymore?

"I once served a knight," he said. "I cannot remember his name."

The girl nodded, still not looking at him. She moved her mouth. "I think that's how it works here," she said and turned to leave, shifting the pitcher to her other arm.

"Goodbye, Squire."

"Goodbye, Missy."

He walked into the shining tent.

A sound like wind chimes rang out overhead, subtle and quiet. Patterns the light made on the ground reminded the Squire of stepping into a forest, perhaps the forest skirting the Timberdrop, but other than the grass under his boots, he saw no green plants. All he saw were walls and walls of mirrors, each one showing back his worried face. He walked for the path deeper in, but bumped into his reflection and followed along with his hand until he found the way again.

A mirror maze. Had he heard of such things before? He thought so. Tales of wizards from the south and their impossible halls came to mind. Legend said only a blind man could find the way through. He couldn't remember if the sorcerer had praised him or ate him... It was hard to figure wizards.

He bumped into another pane of glass. Rubbed his nose.

Surely this wasn't all there was. He looked up, but the glass walls rose high and... stretched back on themselves? The Squire wasn't sure *what* he was looking at. He moved along, keeping his hands outstretched.

He kept a slow pace. Like the rest of this hellish maze, he never found himself at a dead end. It just seemed to go on and on. He lost track of how much time had passed.

After what felt like half a day's trek, he stopped to rest, sitting to lean against a mirror. He looked at his reflection and the boy who stared back was not one he knew.

Filthy, coated in grime and... *blood?* He patted his face but found it dry. Clean even. He remembered washing earlier. Why did the face in the mirror look like he crawled through the gutter of a *blood sport?* He crawled closer, gaping at his reflection.

Cuts covered his face. His hair was long and matted. The clothes he wore were not his own; long, ragged tears showed bruised and purple flesh underneath. He held up his hands. In the reflection, bandages covered one, and the other was missing a few digits. He counted only eight fingers in all.

"*What is this?*" the Squire gasped.

His reflection blinked. "It worked..." it said. "You're separating."

It took a moment for the Squire to realize he hadn't spoken. That his reflection had spoken.

... that his reflection was *speaking*.

He backed away, and the Squire in the mirror *didn't*. The other him looked at his *own* ruined hands and compared them with the Squire's. Wonder filled his eyes.

"Could you... hold your hands up?" he asked.

He was too shocked to not comply. His reflection... Why was his reflection...

The other him laughed, looking between their hands. "*I can't believe it. Is this a farce? Are you real?*" He rapped a knuckle on the face of the mirror. Sounded like the bow-string *twang* of ice shifting on a lake. His reflection smiled wide. Too wide.

"Won't you come closer?" the other him said. "I truly believe we can lend the other aid."

It was his *eyes;* the Squire decided. Something was wrong there, though he couldn't say *what* exactly. Maybe they were too small or too sunken in his head. The Squire backed until he felt the chill of the opposite mirror at his shoulder. His reflection blanched.

"Do you know how *long* I've waited for this?" the thing said. "What I've *done* to get here?"

He hated its voice: so close to his own, but *not*. The reflection slapped the flat of its palm against the glass. "*Are you deaf?*" it said. "We need to leave this place!"

The Squire shook his head. "You're... *wrong.*"

"*I'm* wrong?" the reflection laughed. "*You're* the one in the mirror, friend. What's it like in there? Is it cold?"

The Squire didn't know how to respond, but he knew above all else that he *didn't* want to speak with the thing in the mirror.

The reflection pressed against the mirror, squishing his face flat and wincing at the strain. "It's only... *pain,*" it said and pushed *through*.

The Squire couldn't understand what he was seeing. His reflection—this *thing*—it couldn't be real. Could it*?* But after all the things he'd seen in the maze, what *wasn't* possible?

"You're not real," the Squire said, struggling to believe the words as he spoke them. His reflection looked disgusted.

"You're the one who's *fake*!" it said, spittle flying from its mouth. The mirror burned the Reflection's skin, charring him like the skin of an apple over a fire. The smell of burning flesh overwhelmed him. It was coming *through*...

It was coming through the mirror.

And then a worse thought: *Did every surface here hold a dark reflection?*

He peered over his shoulder to the mirror at his back and locked eyes with the Reflection there. It was the same as the other: battered and scared with alien eyes. It reached to grab him.

"*I'm* real*!*" it yelled. "*Don't resist!*"

The Squire slapped away the singed arm. For the brief moment he touched the Reflection passing through the mirror, he felt a *jolt.* A hot wave of nausea rippled through his gut and he vomited in the grass.

Reflection number two cursed and screamed, while Reflection number one tried where the other had failed, forcing its arm out up to its shoulder.

The Squire crawled, feeling the Reflection's fingers rake uselessly at his leg. Both of them wailed as the Squire escaped.

Don't look at them. Don't look at the mirrors. But how was he supposed to find his way and *not* look? The Blind Man in the story might have found his way, but the Squire didn't have the patience. He needed out *now*.

A hand seized his ankle, and another wretched wave of nausea washed over him.

"*Away!*" he cried and kicked blindly. Something went *snap* behind him and the reflection let loose a wet scream.

They were all around him. Smoking arms flailed from the mirrors, twisted fingers clawing at the shimmering air. Most of them didn't venture far beyond that and those who did dropped writhing on the ground.

The Squire ran through the reaching arms.

When one of them would clench at his collar or swipe at his arm, nausea would bubble up within him and he'd stumble. Scratches marked his neck and limbs. The Reflections all repeated the same thing, "*I'm real!*" over and over, like a desperate chant.

The farther along he ran through the mirrors, the more *different* his reflections became. Here he was older, with greying hair and hollow eyes; and here he was younger, wearing a savage wolf's pelt that burned with *a great* smell as it pressed through the mirror.

The Squire was faster than them, but how long could he keep running? Every mirror created a fresh enemy with fresh life. A sharp pain grew in the Squire's side. He'd collapse from exhaustion before too long, and *then* what? Would these monsters try to pull him through to *their* side?

And then he ran headlong into a mirror—and so—into his reflection, this one the strangest yet.

It was a *puppet*. The Squire carved from wood. As if *he'd* fallen prey to the vile transformation at the manor and *not* his master. It reached through the mirror and the wood burned but was not destroyed. The puppet smiled. "*I'm* real," it said.

The Squire dashed from the grabbing arm and ran
into another mirror.

And another.

Three puppets, the color singed from their bodies, stepped out into the maze and kicked away the other suffering reflections like they were nothing more than twisting snakes on the ground. Thin, blue tendrils of smoke rose from their carved bodies like steam. They smelled of hickory wood.

"*I'm real,*" they said, their voices a strange chorus.

The Squire darted away, paying careful heed to the mirrors. At times, he was a breath away from crashing into another, but he twisted through the maze at a speed he hoped was good enough.

"No dead ends," he breathed. "Never a dead-end... always a way out."

He found another corner, rolled past it...

And froze.

The maze opened in a wide circle. Flowers grew in the grass, spreading out into eternity and vanishing farther and farther away into the mirrors. Sitting in the glade's center was a fountain, the same dark behemoth he'd fallen into all those hours ago.

He ran. So did his other-selves in the mirrors. There might have been forty of them.

The fountain is the way out. The thought came to him as clear as a voice. Crawl into the fountain and he'd be out from the King's clutches. He'd just have to reach it before his puppets.

He would find the Knight and swear to never leave his side again. He'd even be happy to see the snide face of the Rabbit. As he hurried, a little worm of worry in the back of his mind whispered something was wrong, but he didn't have time for it. His hands grasped the rough stone of the fountain just as the first puppet toppled out from its mirror. The Squire looked into the cool water in the fountain's basin and saw...

Himself.

Hands seized his face. The Squire struggled, making waves on the water's surface, making *more* reflections. Hundreds of them took hold of the Squire: some of them whole but most of them only *fractals* of something alive.

They were too strong, and the Squire fell into the water.

THE SPIKE

And out again.

The boy coughed and choked as someone hauled him onto dry ground.

"There you go. Get it all out, don't worry. Don't worry, farmer."

The Squire blinked. He was in a small tent. The wind flapped at its walls and the air was hot. He struggled to focus on Missy as she helped him the rest of the way out of the soapy washing trough.

Soap, that's what this was. It stung his eyes. He coughed until he vomited water. "... *what?*" he gasped.

"Told'ya I'd help." Missy still held the pitcher in one arm. The other one tossed him a towel. "Sorry about your eyes. Had to make do with what I had."

The Squire scrubbed the fire out of his eyes and strained to see. "They're gone?" he said. "Am I... safe here?"

"You're still in the King of Purg's Garden Maze. You're not safe *anywhere*. But yeah. No mirrors in here. You were supposed to pop out somewhere else, but I made a deal with the—"

"I'm still *me?*" the Squire counted the fingers on his hand. Tugged at his hair. Patted the flesh of his face. *Not carved from wood. Not a puppet.*

Missy frowned, considering the question. "Well... the Mirrim takes what we fear of ourselves and makes them real. One of the King's odd little lessons. One most people don't... *live* to appreciate."

The Squire's head was buzzing. He couldn't think. "But... *why?*"

Missy frowned, as if considering the question for the first time. "... I think he's bored? *You* try living a thousand years in your own playground and see how messed up you get. He's basically a vampire without the... You know. *Eating people* gimmick."

He remembered what the Rabbit had said about what had happened to *the rest* of the King's kinsmen.

"Why didn't you warn me about the mirrors?" the Squire asked.

Missy made a face and looked at some distant spot on the floor. "I got you there early, *didn't I?* And I couldn't tell you anything about the Mirrim, because it's against the rules. The Maze doesn't like—"

"So where am I?"

The girl shrugged. "About an hour's walk from the King's tent? The Maze is funny like that. Has its own rules."

"This is a laundry tent," she added quickly. "That's probably what you wanted to know. Should've said that first."

A laundry tent. The Rabbit *had* said to hide, and this was as good a place as any.

Missy said, "So I helped you, *right?* Now you can help me. That was the deal, remember? I know the maze sorta... *helped you* make up your mind about it... but you *did* pinky promise."

"... pinky promise?"

"Yeah. It's like a... magic thing, okay? You'll turn into a frog if you don't follow through."

"That's not how magic works."

"Oh." Missy's face twisted in frustration, like she'd never considered magic being a real enough thing to *have* rules. "Then... how *does* it work?"

"Do I *look* like a magician to you?"

"*Maybe?* I don't know! What does a magician even *look* like?"

Even though the Squire couldn't remember if he had ever met a magician, the image of one sprang into mind easier than the face of his own mother. The suddenness of it frightened him.

"Pray you never know," he said.

"Why?"

"Because they *eat* people."

She shook her head. "Okay, *wow.* I just... I need your help, alright? I promise not to use *cannibal* magic on you, or *whatever* it is. I just wanna get out of here."

All the cuts and scrapes he'd earned over the past day *burned* from the wash-water. Every muscle wanted him to drop to the grassy floor and just *stop*, to drift off into sweet oblivion. He spread out the towel and made to bed down. "*Everybody* wants to get out of here," he said.

"Okay, I *know* you're tired. I know that you just had a hundred evil mirrors try to kill you, but if you stay with me for just a minute more..."

"My friends told me to find a hiding place and *wait.* So that's what I'm going to do."

"Yes, yes, yes—the Rabbit, right?"

He shot to attention.

"You *saw* the Rabbit?"

Missy rocked her head back and forth. "... *sort of?*"

"What does that mean?"

"So," she waved her hand in the air, looking for words, "*you* drank from the King's Fountain—but he *didn't.*"

"The fountain..."

"Yeah. The water sounded musical and tasted sweet? *'Drink and be filled'?* You know what I'm talking about?"

"*Yes,* I know what you're talking about."

"So that's like... the ticket to get in, or something."

"*Ticket?*"

"A scrap of paper that says you can go in a place. *Forget* it. What you need to know is the Rabbit *didn't* drink any. He *can't* find you because he's... not *really* here."

The more she spoke, the more his spirits fell. Was the rabbit here or not? He shook his head. "... what are you talking about?"

"I'm saying you're *deeper* in the maze than he is."

"But then, how did *you* see him?"

"He was throwing pebbles in the water."

The Squire decided not to question further. *Pebbles? Sure.* He rubbed his eyes. "Alright," he said. "If you'd rather me *not* rest, what would you have me do?"

Missy nodded. Shifted the pitcher to her other hip. "The Maze is bound to the King," she said. "*Everything* is at some level, but like glue can get old after a long, long time, the bonds have become *brittle.* The Maze wants to be free of him."

"... the *maze* wants."

"Yes. The Garden Maze of Purg is tired of the King and his games and wants to *rest*."

"You talked to the maze? The tall, thorny bushes?"

"*Just* take my word for it, alright? I don't want to explain every little thing. The point is, if we want to, well... *kill* the King, the maze won't try to stop us."

"You've killed many kings?"

"That's where *you* come in."

"You think *I've* killed many kings?"

Missy threw up a hand. "*I don't know!* You said you served a knight, and you looked tough enough talking to him in his fancy-tent. I thought maybe you were a *hero* or something."

"I'm a *Squire*."

Missy pinched her face and took a breath. She stared up at the canvas ceiling and sighed.

"I don't know how long I've been here," she said. "I don't know if I've lost track of time or if *it's* lost track of *me,* but I know I've been here long enough for people to miss me. New people come into the King's Parade all the time. Some please the King and some don't. Some live and some die... and I'm *jealous*. He's already decided my fate," she lifted the pitcher, "so no life or death choice for me. Just *this*."

"Why *do* you carry that pitcher?"

"Cup."

"Fine, *cup*."

Missy mulled over the answer a moment, like she was thinking up an apology for something broken on the floor. "If I spill a drop, I'll die," she said. "I've thought about pouring the whole thing on his smug face. I'd flicker away, or something. The Maze won't tell *how* I'd die. Against the rules to tell, I think."

She met his eyes, looked difficult for her. "But I don't *want* to give up. I want to *fight*. Sure, I'll probably die anyway, but that's better than giving up!"

The Squire remembered that horrible moment in the coal cellar of the Manor. The *helplessness* of it. If he was going to die, he'd do so with a weapon in his hand. Not that he *had* a weapon. The Knight had the sword, and the Rabbit had his bow... the Squire could throw a rock well enough.

The Squire said, "If this is what you want, then finding my friends would be a great asset to your cause. We had much the same plan as you, but we were counting on my master being the one to land the killing blow—on account of him recently becoming difficult to kill."

Missy frowned. "And how *did* you plan to kill the King?"

"*Stabbing* is usually an effective way to stop someone breathing. We figured we'd try that."

"Yes, but with *what?*"

The Squire shrugged. "My master has a blade we'd bring upon him. It's sharp and true. More than what we need."

But Missy shook her head. "Maybe where you come from it would be enough, but in his domain, only a weapon crafted of the Maze can slay him. Here..."

She stretched her hand over the ground, and a savage spine rose from the dirt. A thorn from the hedge maze, but *gargantuan*. It looked weaved from *countless* thorns all twisted into one. The tip looked sharp enough to pierce the plated armor of a direworm. It grew three feet before Missy knelt to pluck it from the grass. She passed it to the Squire.

"*This* should kill him," she said.

He took the Spike. The wood of the hilt was smooth and molded *perfectly* for his grip. It was heavier than it should have been, but not in a bad way. *This is such a blade that would please my master,* he thought.

Then the mournful sound of a horn drifted through the air and Missy's attention snapped toward the tent flap. She shook her head, confused. "They couldn't have found a new group so *soon*..."

But then the horn sounded again and again. Her face flattened.

"What?" the Squire said. "Does it mean something? What's wrong *now*?"

She moved her mouth to the side. Blinked. "What exactly made your knight friend hard to kill?" she asked.

"It was the puppets. They... made him drink a potion."

"Puppets?"

The horn let loose another round of mournful blasts. They were closer now and Missy's face betrayed her worry. "That can't mean anything good," she said.

Movement outside. Someone creeping close. The Squire held firm his grip on the Spike.

They both nearly bowled over backward when the Rabbit burst through the tent flap. His fur was dripping and his eyes held that mad look the Squire had come to recognize. Something had gone wrong. It took some time before the Rabbit caught his breath again.

"... never seen... such *idiocy*... in all my days..."

Missy stared down at him, curiosity in her eye. "You drank from the fountain," she said.

"*Yes*, I drank from the *damned fountain!* No thanks to *you*." He marched for the Squire. "Listen *carefully*. Your idiot master thought he'd try to sneak into the Parade to find you."

"You found a way around?"

The Rabbit sputtered. "No, we fell asleep eating cake under a *fairy tree* and woke up here. *OF COURSE WE FOUND THE WAY AROUND, YOU LOW-BORN FOOL!* Are you just balancing that head between your shoulders, or is it *actually attached*?"

"Just tell me what happened!"

The Rabbit smiled wickedly. "Of course. The King's guards have taken into custody our dear friend, Mr. Puppet while he set off searching *for you*."

"Why didn't you *stop him?*"

The Rabbit shook his head, still smiling. "Oh *dear, dear, dear*. If only I had *thought of that*. Were only I as wise as *you*."

The Squire didn't know what to say. Talking to the Rabbit was like bashing your head against a post. The more you did, the more confused you became. He tossed up his arms. "So, what now?"

"Nothing has changed," the Rabbit said. "It has only become *harder*. What is that you hold?" The Rabbit sniffed the weapon in the Squire's hand and blinked in surprise. "Made from the Maze, is it?"

"Yes," Missy said.

The Rabbit regarded her for the first time, his eyes sharp. "You're the *water girl*, aren't you?" He hopped her way and regarded the pitcher in her grasp, very careful not to touch it. "*Oh*, this is ancient. I've only seen one such before. It was in my collection before the idiot *boy* destroyed it."

The Squire frowned. "I don't remember seeing a pitcher in the gallery."

"My *painting*, boy! It was the same as this cup: charmed by the Ancients of Purg. This very well might be the last of—"

Missy broke him from his lecture. "Mr. Rabbit, I hate to interrupt..."

The Rabbit nodded. "Yes. *Yes*. As I said, the plan is the same as before. Get close to the King and end him with that Spike. Good for you to have found it. I was hoping the King would keep something like it nearby, like a trophy or something of the like."

"The Maze gave it to us," Missy said.

The Rabbit laughed. "Spoken like a true child! And that is not a criticism. Oh no, you'll need that good 'old fashion sunshine and *naivete* where we're going. The fool boy *especially*."

The Squire had had *enough*. He jabbed a finger at the Rabbit's buttoned vest. "You watch your words. I've gotten this far, haven't I?"

"And you have further yet to go! We're down a knight, remember? So take a guess at who gets the honor of challenging the King?"

THE ROSES

Orc-men stood at arms around the King's tent. Each ready to draw swords nearly as long as the Squire himself. They scanned the grounds with their emerald eyes and spotted the Missy and the Squire instantly.

Missy pushed him walking again and called to the orc-men. "He survived the Mirrim after all. The Maze decided to—"

"The King is not to be disturbed," the orc-man said. He glowered from behind his silver mask. "You're to move along, *water girl.*"

Missy frowned, her mouth twitching to one side as she studied the roses on the side of the tent, never looking directly at the guard. "This is a very special guest," she said. "He's... *special.*"

The Rabbit thumped the small of the Squire's back from his hiding place in his shirt. "*Help her!*" he hissed.

The Squire opened his mouth. "He... told me to return if I—"

The orc-man knelt on one knee and looked the Squire level in the face. The Squire could smell his boggy breath with every *puff.* He said, "Boy should not speak. He should *listen,* and rabbit hiding listen too."

(the Rabbit *harrumphed* from his hiding place)

"The King is in a bad sort," the orc-man said. "Sight of the puppet man made him angry. If boy, girl, and rabbit go in *now,* your lives are forfeit. I heard him speak of the *roses.*"

Much to the Squire's annoyance, the Rabbit wriggled his head up through his collar. His ears bopped against his face.

"Do you hate the King?" the Rabbit asked.

The orc-man remained silent, his green eyes aglow. He looked at the other orc-men standing guard, but they gave neither sign they heard nor cared. "I *serve* the King," he said at last.

The Squire dumped the Rabbit out of his shirt. He landed lightly on his feet.

"*We* hate the King," the Rabbit said waving to the other two. "Our friend inside does as well. Perhaps it would please the King to have us all in one place when he calls for the Roses?"

The orc-man stared at the Rabbit... at the Squire and the girl. He rose to his full height, drawing his sword. "This *may* please the King," he said.

"Of course, I wouldn't want to trouble *you* with leading us inside. In case we displease the King."

The orc-man stepped aside. "Yes, this is wise," he said and used the tip of his sword to lift the tent's wall. He looked at the other guards, but none of them made any move against them.

"You should move *faster,*" the orc-man said.

The Squire and Rabbit wasted no time, but Missy needed some help to get through without spilling from her pitcher.

The Squire leaned to help her balance the weight, but she nearly fell over, dodging him.

"You can't touch it!" she said. "Or *you'll* have to carry the King's cup."

The orc-man and Squire lifted the tent high enough for her to carry it inside. When the way out dropped closed behind them, the Rabbit rubbed his hands together.

"I've only been here once before," he said. "Many, many years ago." They were behind a partition. From deeper in, they could hear voices.

"You can tell us all about it later," the Squire said. "For now, if you could simply show the way?"

The Rabbit straightened his vest and looked to Missy. "Does his throne still face East?" he asked.

Missy furrowed her brow and bit her lip. "... huh."

"*You don't know which...*" the Rabbit shut his mouth and pointed. "*That* is north," he said slowly, "Therefore, *thaaaat way*,"

"Okay, yes, Or... *no*—in answer to your question. The throne doesn't face east anymore. *West* now, I guess."

"West..." This seemed to disturb the Rabbit. He took a little more time aligning his buttons. "Strange, that. Water Girl, could you collect that sword again?"

They had returned it to the ground to better sneak into the King's tent. But Missy had assured them she could call it forth from the Garden again. She did so now, "It's a Spike," she said, and once more the dark weapon slid up through the sod and into the Squire's hand.

He felt *better* holding it in his grip. Even though he still had doubts about facing the King... he wagered with the Spike, he'd at least have a *glimmer* of a chance.

"Let's see what's behind this curtain," the Rabbit whispered.

A single table dominated the space. Food of every shape and kind had been set upon it, the aroma rising like an intoxicating steam. An unlit chandelier hung dead above it; providing nothing but shadows for the banquet. In what little light allowed, the table seemed to be... moving. *Twisting.*

Then the Squire's eyes adjusted and he saw the shapes for what they were. Spiny tendrils inched around the dishes and saucers, looping around serving spoons and scratching at the puckered skin of roasted lamb and strings of pheasants. Red rose petals littered the ground.

The Squire stepped upon a carpet of deepest blue, his bare feet sinking into warmth. Missy pulled at his arm to stay, but he pressed into the room, not staring at the living rosebush exploring the table, but at those who sat at either end.

The Duke of Purg and the Viscount of Velay started at their sudden entry.

Their skin was pale, as if they'd spent many days away from the sun in some pit. Sweat dotted their faces, though the room was cool. And though the Squire had caught the Duke's eye, the man kept his focus on the table and the thriving rose bush upon it.

The Squire had seen an octopus once. He couldn't remember the circumstance, but the sight of the roses overflowing on the table brought the slinking creature to mind.

The Viscount lifted a finger. "*Who is that?*" he asked. He searched the room with empty eyes, aged to the color of milk.

How many days had it been since he'd seen the Viscount? Beholding the man's doughy face and searching eyes after all this time was a shock the Squire hadn't expected. The fat man frowned like someone had played a cruel trick on him in the dark.

"Don't treat an old man, so," he said. "Who goes there?"

It was with another shock that the Squire noticed the deep wrinkles in the man's fat face and the white wisps of his hair.

The Duke, however, looked just as he had when the Squire had first laid eyes on him, when the Knight had throttled the viper in his dark tent. The Duke spoke up, never moving his gaze from the heavy vines. "It is *no one*, my old friend. Simply the wind. *Eat!* The servants have set the table with all manner of goods."

But the Viscount shook his head. "There is a vile taste under my tongue. I feel as if I am in the shadow of a malicious spirit and I cannot bid to leave." His empty eyes roved in vain. "*Speak*," he said. "*Please*, who is there?"

The vines crept closer to the Viscount, spreading tendrils over the arms of his chair. The Squire ignored the Rabbit pulling him from the scene and moved for the banquet.

"Lord Viscount," he said.

The fat man jolted as if struck. "*Your voice*," he wailed, "I know your voice, but I cannot name it!"

The vines on the table grew agitated. A dish toppled and crashed to the floor, speckling dark gravy over their feet. The Duke's fingers gripped at his chair till they turned white. Sweat held his hair against his brow. "Nothing to fear, dear Viscount. It is merely a slave of the house. Pay him no heed."

"But I know his voice!"

"Simply the imagining of an old mind." The Duke turned his eyes from the table and gave the Squire a dark look. His pale face stretched, lips curling with a flash of teeth like a cat hissing from a trash heap. The sight forced the boy a step back.

The Duke snapped, "The boy should be about his duties. Not bothering our honored guest as he enjoys his evening meal."

The Viscount turned again for the table, his face a mask of sorrow. "I had friends, once," he said. "*True* friends. I was a fool and traded them away."

The roses looped their vines around the Viscount's arm, but the man seemed not to notice. Meanwhile, the thorns were exploring the Duke's end of the banquet. One tendril stretched lazily for his chair. The Duke kept still. "*Please*," he said, his voice almost a whisper. "Have something to eat."

The Squire paced closer to his old master. "My Lord," he said. "The Knight and I went into the Garden Maze of Purg at your behest. Do you remember?"

"He lies," the Duke said, lips hardly moving as the roses crept *closer*.

"The Knight of *Norland*," the Viscount breathed. "Father's old protector."

A vine crossed the divide to the Duke. A thorn kissed his thumb.

With a blast, the Duke tore from his chair. The man's legs *spun* in his panic to flee the table, but the Roses were faster. The creature erupted and threw the feast to the floor. Again, the vision of an octopus rose to mind as the tendrils found the Duke's body. Vines enveloped him.

The Roses had chosen their meal and the tendrils exploring the Viscount's chair pulled away in a violent rush, causing it to topple. The Squire jumped to catch his old master as he fell, but the weight proved too great.

The chair toppled and the Viscount, his face fearful and confused, fell to the ground with a thud. He groaned, clutching at his chest as his blind eyes wobbled in their sockets. The Squire took his hand and found it cold.

The fingers gripped his. "I found... very little, in my life," the Viscount said, "I hope you... find *more*," and breathed his last.

Here was the man the Squire and Knight had detested so fiercely. The tottering oaf who spent his days hanging on others' arms as he reached for his next drink. How often had the Knight spoken of being rid of him?

Yet he felt tears wetting his face.

The Rabbit came to his side. "*Are you mad?*" he hissed and pulled at his shirt like the boy had wandered into the open mouth of a lion. "*Leave this place while we can!*"

The Roses had drug the Duke beneath the table. He struggled no longer. The vines constricted with a noise like vultures ripping into carrion. This close to the dreaded thing, the Squire could feel sweat bead on his face and neck. The Rabbit pulled at his arm.

"*Move before it looks for dessert!*"

With one last look at his old master, the Squire chased after Missy and the Rabbit, out into the halls of the King's tent.

For such a large place, there were very few people in it. As they walked down the glowing hall, the Squire held his breath and listened for life.

It was the manor all over again, but instead of a dark house, it's a bright temple!

The Rabbit led the way, leaving the Squire and Missy to keep a weary eye to the rear in case the Roses followed after. He walked with his hands placed behind his back and spine straight—his *curator* persona taking charge.

As they went, the Squire gazed up into the tent's red, vaulted heights. Again, he wondered just how *big* the place could be. The Maze didn't seem to follow the rules of left & right, and up & down.

Missy leaned to whisper. "*He must be very angry.*"

"What?"

"The King. This place gets *bigger* when he's angry. I've never seen this hall stretched so long."

The Rabbit shushed her. His ears quivered in the air as he stared ahead, sniffing the air. "We're *close*," he said. A sudden quiver had come into his voice. "Each of you must remain *perfectly* silent. If the King senses us near, we'll have only *moments* to act."

The Squire renewed his grip on the Spike. If they were lucky, they'd find the King facing away when they entered. And if not? Well... *speed* would be an ally.

"I can go in ahead of you," Missy said. "I'll get him facing the right way."

The Rabbit blinked. "And which direction would that be, *lovey?*"

Missy glared at the Rabbit, her mouth a thin line. "I think *away from you* should be good enough."

The Rabbit smiled. "For now, yes," and led them to another partition, identical to hundreds of others they had passed on their way. He placed a paw upon the fabric like it was a beast geared to explode. He looked back at them, eyes wide. *Here,* he mouthed.

The Rabbit and Squire padded away as Missy steeled herself to enter. She shot them a sidelong glance, scrunched her face, and waved them off a few paces more. The Squire gripped the thorn with popping knuckles.

Go on, the Rabbit nodded.

He didn't want to watch. He wanted to close his eyes, to look away, but the Squire crouched were he was. His muscles tensed—whether to rush with aid or flee in shame, he couldn't say. He could only stare at Missy's hand as she reached to push aside the blood-red curtain.

As soon as she did, the effect was immediate.

Sound blasted them, making the Squire jump as if he'd broken the early morning quiet with the *crash* of a glass bowl.

The King was shouting at someone. So enraged was his voice, the Squire couldn't make sense of the words. But as soon as Missy stepped past the curtain and into the room beyond, the King's mouth shut with an audible click. From where he stood, the Squire could still see her through the sliver of the curtain. He saw only the edge of her face, but he could read the panic there as she stared ahead. Her free hand still held to the curtain's edge, fingers tense, her last hope of escape.

All was still. Quite swallowed the earth.

At last, the King spoke. His voice the picture of calm. "Did I call for you, child?" he asked. "You look afraid. Don't be. He can't hurt anyone. Can you, sir knight?"

The Squire heard a *click*, like a horse-hoof striking a stone.

"Come in," the King said. "It's alright."

Missy's fingers flinched and lost their hold on the curtain. The heavy fabric fell into place once more, and the room beyond vanished. The Squire stepped away. Goblins were clawing in his stomach and he suddenly felt *very* cold. He pulled his hair.

"*This isn't going to work!*" he said. "I can't do this!"

"*Shut up, shut up, shut up!*" the Rabbit hissed. "We'll give her a little time and then you *run in* and drive that Spike into his chest."

The Squire's hands shook. His master was behind that curtain, and the King of Purg was doing who knows *what* to him. He thought of the Viscount, left dead on the floor. They'd *never* get out of here. Never escape. His heart was beating too fast... too fast...

The Rabbit hopped up and kicked his chest. The Squire stumbled back, landing soundly on his rump.

"You *listen!*" The Rabbit said and pointed. "*I* can't do it. Your hapless *Knight* can't do it, and little *Missy* can't let a *drop* fall from her burden or the Garden *itself* will rip her into cuts of meat for the Roses. It must be *you!*"

The Squire took a breath. One last time, he tried to *remember*. If he was going to die, he wanted to hold a happy thought in his mind before the end, but all the Maze allowed him was sorrow.

A night drenched in rain.
A promise broken outside a nameless city wall.
Dust in his teeth. The smell of rot in his nose.
Nightmares of wolves. Howling.

It was like the Maze itself had eaten him away, bit by bit. Taking a little here and there... stealing his life, his mind, his happiness... He'd been a happy child once, *hadn't he?* He thought so. Hoped so.

The Rabbit took hold of the Spike and pricked his paw on the sharpened tip. He stretched out his fingers and showed the Squire. Blood the same color as the hallways towering around them dripped from his palm. The Rabbit showed his teeth. "It's *sharp*," he said. "That's all you need!"

He looked one last time at the Spike in his hand, feeling its weight. A gift from the Maze.

The Squire strode through the curtain.

Missy lay on her belly, her arms quivering as she held the Pitcher aloft. The King had his foot planted between her shoulders, resting most of his weight on her spine. Missy's face was white, her eyes closed.

The Pitcher wobbled.

"*Ah!*" the King shouted, a smile stretching across his face. He lifted his hands in the air. "*Congratulations* my young Squire! You bested the Mirrim and its tricks. *All by yourself.*"

Missy shook as the King shifted his weight. He brought a finger to his chin.

"In fact... I've never seen *anyone* run it that quickly. Nobody lent you a hand, did they?"

The Squire froze. The Spike in his hand felt *woefully* small. *He's killing her. He'll break her back or she'll break the pitcher.*

Then he saw what stood behind the king and all strength left his legs.

He had twisted the Knight into a post. He could see his arms and his legs, but only by their seams. They'd been wrapped 'round and 'round his body in knots and cords, far beyond their natural length. Only his face, though frozen in a sorrowful gaze, was untouched by disfigurement. The only hint of life looked out with one mournful eye. The Knight blinked a heavy blink and beheld the Squire.

"*Master,*" the Squire gasped, tears flowing over his face. The Spike clattered to the golden flecked marble.

The King of Purg turned to look at the Knight. "Like the craftsmanship?" he asked. "I thought I'd leave it by the entry there. Have something for guests to hang their coats."

The Squire tried again to remember the Knight as he had been. Strained to bring to mind even one *snatch* of memory, but the King had taken it all. As the monster stood there before the husk of his master, he seemed to glow; forever young and forever victorious.

Then the Rabbit darted like a wildcat.

He snatched the Spike from the floor with a musical *scratch!* and leaped for the King with eyes like twin fires and teeth bared in a primal scream.

The Spike whistled through the air.

But it whistled louder when the King swung his arm and struck the Rabbit with a dreadful *crunch*. His body flung to the far side of the room and the Spike clattered to rest beside him.

And that was all Missy could bear. She cried out in pain and terror as the pitcher tumbled from her grasp,

and into the Squire's.

For a moment, all time froze. The air buzzed with power and all was still.

Then a laugh began in the King's chest. It rose, stretching wilder and stranger as the man's voice filled the tent. He kicked Missy out from under his feet and *howled*. "Yes, *YES!*" he screamed. "*It's only fair!*"

A weight filled the Squire's arms, but not from the cup (*for of course, it was a cup*). Something else was here... something *besides* water and sculpted clay.

Missy sat on the ground, both her hands shaking before her. She looked to the Squire, open shock coloring her face. "*It's gone,*" she said.

The King stopped his laughter to grin down at them. A red line shone out across his face, from the corner of his smiling mouth to ear. Blood seeped through like paint through a seam. The Rabbit had hit his mark, but only just.

"It's not *gone*, dear child," he said. "It has simply changed hands."

"You told me—"

"I told you a *lot* of things. Some of them were true and some of them were *more* than true because I *said so*." He gestured to the pitcher in the Squire's hand. "This burden cannot be shared unless *forced*. I did you a favor when I lied, for you did not know its true weight and could therefore pass it on without guilt."

He smiled, blood streaming down his chin as his eye moved to the Squire. "*But not a gift I shall give to you,*" he hissed. He dipped a finger into the vessel's water and let it drizzle from his hand. "It's all our hope you hold, boy. The ancients of Purg bound the power of the earth on which we stand to the water in this... very... cup. To pour it out is to bring about the freedom of *all... but,*" his breath was hot in the Squire's ear, "will only grant *damnation* for yourself."

The King stood to his full height. Blood from his face had stained the neck of his robe. "I have one criterion when letting fools into *my* Maze. Care to guess?"

The Squire's mouth was dry. When he gazed into the cup, no reflection looked back to greet him. He didn't know what that could mean.

The King's voice resounded in his empty chamber. "*Self-ishness!* The Maze *sifts* for it, killing any who prove to be loyal to any but themselves."

Missy shook her head. "N... no. I'm not... I'm..."

The King pursed his lips. "The dog liked your sister better than you, didn't it? Couldn't have *that*. And where are *they now?*"

She couldn't look the Squire in the face.

"The choice is yours," the King said. He strolled to where the Rabbit lay motionless and took up the Spike. He *whipped* it through the air, relishing the noise. "You can end everything *right now*. Just dash that pitcher to the ground and embrace *oblivion*! The Maze and every soul in it will be free. And you? *Well*, you'll end up like Mr. Coatrack over there."

The Squire looked once more to his master. His face remained as it was, his eye *fixed* on him.

I could end the madness. End all this suffering. I could do it.

His lips shook as the realization came. He doubled his grip around the cup, holding it close to his body as an angry cry shook his throat. Hot tears burned his face.

He couldn't do it. How could he? It wasn't fair to ask this of him! He could feel Missy's eyes. Was she waiting for him to upend the cup, or would she rush to push him and watch the pottery shatter? He thought back to the woman in the cage, the feeling of her clawing fingers on his arm, eager to trade him for her own life.

But then he thought of himself in that cage. His own hands reaching out, dirty and broken. He saw as much in the Mirrim, all his reflections scratching for blood to take their place.

He thought. *If you had known, would you have caught it?* He was afraid he knew the answer.

The King admired the Spike, swishing it through the air and smiling at the sound. "It's amazing to be the King of the weak," he said.

A noise filled the room.

Small at first, but then growing in strength. For a moment, The Squire feared the Maze itself was changing as it had before, the walls folding and collapsing on themselves in thunderous chaos. But that had been a *different* sound. What he heard now was the breaking and splintering of...

Wood.

A new pair of hands took hold of the pitcher. All in the room spun to see the Knight, folding and unfolding the great length of his arms as his fingers snapped like brittle wood around the Cup.

The King's face dropped in horror, color draining away. His legs wobbled as he strode toward and away from the Knight. His mouth lulled. Spittle flew from his lips. "*No,*" he said. "*You are a selfish old man. A coward. You would not...*"

The Knight didn't bother the King with a gaze. Instead, he kept his sight fixed upon the Squire, a tear wobbling in his eye.

The King screamed, a terror filling his throat as the Knight lifted the cup—his arms cracking like trees in a hurricane—and poured the clear water over his head.

The earth *jumped*.

Thunder blasted through the air with a force unlike the Squire had ever known.

The King howled like a beast, clawing at the Knight's wooden body until his hands were bloody mitts. All around them, Roses broke through the marble, like fingers poking through a rotted cloth.

Missy grabbed hold of the Squire's hand. "*RUN!*" she screamed. Together, they fled from the King of Purg's tent as the Roses took it.

The Parade was chaos. All those beautiful and horrible tents were shaking like hulking beasts had taken hold of their foundations. People ran in panic; the Squire and the girl running along with them.

The Roses snaked from the earth to take one person and to leave another. Again and again, the Squire was sure he'd feel the stinging *bite* of thorns and he'd fall and be drug into the earth to be crushed or mauled or *whatever* these devil flowers decided was to be done with him, but the moment never came.

The great walls of the Garden maze shook as they ran. Before they could reach them, those walls bowed and twisted, shrinking away until only a clear, *straight* path remained.

Their feet *flew*, and the walls passed them in great *rushes*. The dark, drooping flowers that had fogged their minds were choked and tossed down by the Roses. The way before them *opened* and *opened* until it felt like they were *falling*, not running.

Tears stung at the Squire's eyes. As the maze *moved* around them, memories returned in floods.

The flash of color in a world of grey as a man tossed an apple to a little boy on the street.

A song sung on the road as the gentle rain pattered upon his rain-slick.

Groggy from too early a morning, gazing through the crisp air of the Timberdrop mountain to behold the first sunrise of spring.

And the Knight, as he had been so long ago. The man who'd slain the wolves and taught him how to set a campfire.

He couldn't see for all the tears flooding his eyes. Missy kept them straight or else they would have fallen into the river of thorns at either side. And *still*, the Maze moved, moved, *moved*.

Then all was still. And quiet.

They stood at the stone the Duke had led them to all that time ago. The Squire could smell the salt of the nearby sea in the night air and the moon overhead was the smallest of slivers. He stared up at it, wiping his face with his sleeve.

"It... let us go," he said. "The Maze. The roses didn't take us."

Missy could only nod, gazing up at the night sky with tears of her own. "It's been so long," she sobbed. "I forgot... how wonderful..." She dropped into the prickly grass and laughed.

For a moment, they were still. They breathed deep the cool... *Autumn* air? The Squire wasn't sure. The Century Fair was always held in the Spring, but the air held too much chill for—

The Squire searched for lantern lights. He should smell *wood smoke* and *cooking* in the night air, not the ocean. But the Century Fair was nowhere to be seen. Not even stray trash or the embers of a dying fire. It was *long* gone. *Trees* stood where the pennants of the noble houses once flew. It was a *forest now*. The Squire stared, mouth agape.

Missy followed his gaze and tilted her head. "*I* don't recognize any of this," she said. "What about you? Did you get your memories back?"

The Squire laughed. Some had returned, but not all. But he had a feeling more would come. Little by little.

"Do you know what's over there?" Missy asked.

The Squire shook his head. "I don't know. Let's go see."

They walked into the dark forest, and the trees moved to cover them.

ACKNOWLEDGMENTS

Thank you for reading The Garden Maze. It was a labour of love and I can't wait to show all of you what's next. As with every book, it took more than just one person to see it through to completion. I'd like to thank Dylan Frostad, for his editing and advice (I hope you're ready for Song of Bones), as well as my brother Josh for his beautiful cover and putting up with my pedantic lighting suggestions. I'd also like to thank my family as a whole for encouraging me to see this endeavor through to the end and reading all my messy first and second drafts.

Until next time.

www.ingramcontent.com/pod-product-compliance
Lightning Source LLC
Chambersburg PA
CBHW051120300726